THE LAST TEXT YOU SENT

Elise Fender

www.BOROUGHSPUBLISHINGGROUP.com

THE LAST TEXT YOU SENT
Copyright © Elise Fender

ISBN 978-1-953810-97-7

In loving memory of my brother, NRF

ACKNOWLEDGMENTS

First and foremost, thank you, beautiful reader for reading my debut novel. I've been writing this book for many years, and it's a joy to know it is in your hands.

The Last Text You Sent is dedicated to the memory of my brother, Nick. I couldn't have possibly written this story without knowing what it's like to love your brother and to lose him too soon.

Thank you, Nick for twenty-two years of inside jokes, sibling shenanigans, and beautiful memories. I miss you.

Thank you to my agent, Katie Salvo and Metamorphosis Literary Agency for believing in me, and giving me a chance. I appreciate your hard work, and exceptional kindness.

Thank you to my editor and the top-notch team at Boroughs Publishing Group.

Thank you to all my early readers for your wisdom and encouragement. Ansley, you were one of the first people I trusted to read *The Last Text You Sent*, and your opinion meant the world to me. Thank you for supporting me in every way possible from Costco runs to contract advice.

Lynda, you've been a creative inspiration in my life for twenty-five years. Thank you for decades of friendship and for being an early reader of *The Last Text You Sent*. Most importantly, thank you for letting me borrow Grandma Brown's story. I hope I did her love of Elvis justice.

Megan, thank you for thoughtful edits and insight into the world of cross-country runners.

Thank you to all my colleagues, and thank you to our amazing graduate residents. I appreciate your support and encouragement.

Thank you to my whole Fredericksburg tribe. Being surrounded by beautiful, smart, funny women is what inspired me to finish my book. Special thanks to Paige for driving my babies to school every single morning. I love you all and cherish your friendship.

Thank you to my mom, who was my first writing teacher. Thank you to my dad, who taught me everything I know about working hard and never giving up. Thank you, Wren, Knox, and Eden for being my whole world.

Over the past year, a lot of people have asked me how I manage to write with three small children at home. It's a one-word answer: Scott. Scott who cooked dinner every single night, and made me coffee every single morning. Thank you for teaching me about brains, and reading my story to make sure all the science was correct. I love you, and I love the little team we've built together.

THE LAST TEXT YOU SENT

CHAPTER ONE

Tuesday, December 21ˢᵗ

I didn't come to this bonfire party to drink beer or have fun. I came for one reason and one reason only. I'm looking for someone. A specific someone. Someone who has four initials: OCMC. I imagine the "OC" is probably a super Southern double name. This isn't exactly a lot of information to go on, but I don't really have a choice. I have to figure out who OCMC is, and I need to do it soon so I can finally clear things up and set the record straight.

Margot has no clue why I wanted to tag along to the party tonight. I'm sure she hates having her awkward younger cousin here. But she couldn't say no. She pities me like everybody else does. Margot had one condition for me coming tonight: she insisted on "dressing me" so I wouldn't embarrass her with my normal athleisure style. That's how I ended up standing on this red park bench in heeled black ankle booties instead of my usual Chucks.

I scan the crowd and see a group of local teens drinking and laughing. All of them are wearing happy, festive Santa hats or sparkly headbands. Scanning this crowd kind of makes me miss being a normal seventeen-year-old.

I'm not sure exactly what it is I'm looking for. I guess I'm hoping to spot a girl who looks like she has the initials OCMC. Maybe she'll be wearing one of those prissy monogrammed fleeces. Or maybe she'll have on a number eight football jersey. It's not impossible.

After all, she was in love with my brother, Whit, the infamous number eight.

I continue to scan the crowd, but I've yet to spot someone with OCMC tattooed on her forehead. Margot's heeled boots are starting to murder my feet, so I take a break to sit on the bench. I run my fingers on the red metal weave pattern of the bench and realize I'm having a Proustian moment.

One silver lining to this shitty situation is I now know words like "Proustian." Since I spent all my waking hours reading about brain trauma after the accident, I learned about Marcel Proust. Proust wrote about how tiny things, like a red bench, can trigger big memories. In my case, this bench is bringing me right back to my first kiss.

Riley, my best friend back home in Nashville, says the kiss doesn't count. I only grazed lips with the boy, and I didn't even learn his last name. Plus, I haven't seen him in the four years since the kiss happened. All these facts add up to a "non-kiss" in Riley's book.

Anytime we talk about my pathetic love life, Riley loves to bring it up. "You've basically never been kissed," Riley always says. "You can't say Violin Jack was your first kiss. It doesn't count if there's no tongue, you know." Riley coined the term "Violin Jack" when we were thirteen and I proudly told her the story of my first kiss.

I was here in Black Mountain, NC for summer vacation and was taking a walk around this very park when I heard the *Doctor Who* theme song floating through the summer air. I turned around and spotted a boy around my age, sitting on one of the red benches lining the park. He was strumming out the bum-bum-bum-bums of the *Doctor Who* theme on a violin. I didn't have enough courage to strike up a conversation with a random boy (I still don't), but he was playing the violin (not an intimidating instrument) and was clearly a *Doctor Who* fan, my all-time favorite show. Riley and I binge it any time it rains. I managed to eke out an awkward hello, followed by a compliment about his playing. We started chatting and walking through the park.

His name was Jack, he was tall and skinny like a beanpole, and had an Elvis Presley keychain dangling from his violin case. When I told him I needed to get home, he leaned in and kissed me lightly and sweetly on the lips before turning away in embarrassment.

I never saw Jack again, and never learned his last name. But the legend of Violin Jack and my *Doctor Who*-inspired first kiss lives on in infamy.

My Proustian moment passes, but the aching in my feet doesn't. I'm going to have to push through this pain though because I have only two weeks left in Black Mountain and I can't leave this town without finding OCMC.

I can't go back to Nashville until I figure out what secret Whit was keeping from me. I stand up on the bench and start scanning the crowd again, even more determined this time.

I spot two pretty girls draped over an effortlessly cool boy playing a guitar. Both girls are wearing way too much makeup. I can tell they'd be pretty even without the piles of clumpy mascara. I say a quiet prayer neither of them turn out to be OCMC. They have cigarettes dangling from their cotton-candy-pink-glossed lips, and they're wearing tops that show off their ample fake tanned cleavage.

Margot always says "all townie girls are skanks" in Black Mountain. I've told her that's wrong on multiple levels, but these two girls aren't exactly helping my argument.

One of the townie girls is sitting on Guitar Guy's knee, and the other has her hands draped over his muscular back. His head is down, and his long, shaggy black hair is hanging over his eyes. He's big, built, and looks more like somebody I would expect to see on Whit's football team than playing an instrument.

For a boy who has fawning girls with their hands all over him, he sure plays the guitar well. He's strumming out "Jingle Bells" but he's adding Johnny Cash vibes to the tune.

Guitar Guy looks up as he sings "ho, ho, ho" and our gazes meet.

I stare, and he stares back.

I hold his gaze for a moment longer before I realize *he's Violin Jack.*

CHAPTER TWO

I look down at my throbbing feet and hope he doesn't recognize me. I'm painfully aware the first boy I ever kissed morphed from a skinny beanpole music nerd into a full-on muscle-bound, bad-boy heartthrob. On the other hand, I'm standing awkwardly on a bench in a borrowed outfit that doesn't fit me, probably looking as cringey as I feel.

Violin Jack has grown up, and I've faded into a shriveled brown weed.

I step off the bench, keeping my head down, praying he isn't still looking at me. I find my way back to Margot and her circle of townie friends. I must look as shaken as I feel because Margot actually checks in. "You cool? You look like you're going to like...hurl."

"I'm cool," I lie. "Hey, do you know that boy over there with the guitar?" I point at Violin Jack, trying to sound nonchalant.

Margot looks at him then wrinkles her nose. "That's Jack. Total townie freak," she says.

The boy with his arm draped around Margot echoes her opinion. "Don't mess with that guy. He's a shitshow."

Despite the warning, I still consider approaching the little guitar circle. But when I play it out in my head, the whole thing feels comical. What exactly would I say to Violin Jack and his girlfriends? I've barely talked to another human besides Riley in weeks. Do I really think I could march up to some strangers and ask if any of them ever boned my brother? Suddenly, why I'm here feels utterly pathetic.

I turn on the uncomfortable wedge boots and start walking back toward my gran's mountain cottage. I walk as fast as Margot's expensive shoes will carry me. I don't even bother telling her I'm leaving. I doubt she'll care. She seems right at home among the other effortlessly smooth and normal teenagers.

I am about a block from the bonfire party when I hear heavy footsteps behind me. It occurs to me that nobody knows my whereabouts. It's dark and I'm alone.

My parents couldn't possibly survive more bad news. My mind darts to where it always does lately: if the owner of the heavy footsteps murders me, what would be the last text my parents find on my phone?

I think. Probably me to Riley: *Say a lil' prayer I find OCMC tonight.*

I'm ready to start sprinting to safety when I hear a deep, gravelly voice. "Don't I know you from somewhere?"

I stop and turn. Violin Jack. In the flesh. Standing a mere five yards away. He's wearing a white t-shirt, leather jacket, and old torn-up jeans. His guitar strap is hanging coolly over his shoulder amidst his long black hair. He has a cigarette perched between his lush lips. When I describe him to Riley later tonight, I imagine using words like "chiseled" and "cowboy." I am too paralyzed to answer him.

He shouts again. "Hey, you. I think I know you."

"No, you don't," I squeak out and then I keep walking because I can't think of anything more embarrassing than this moment. But I'm wrong. It gets worse.

"I really feel like I know you. But I can't remember your name," he shouts.

It's at this exact moment I feel the weight of the past few weeks hit me. All the changes I hate and can't control run through my mind. Everything I once knew to be true has crumbled around me. If everything has changed, why am I still clinging to my life as the quiet girl in the shadows? What the hell do I have to lose?

I snap. "Are you frickin' kidding me? Are you for real?" I scream and gesture erratically with my arms, and I'm sure I look as unhinged as I feel. "This is the absolute cherry on top of the world's shittiest Christmas vacation. The first boy I ever kissed doesn't even remember my name. That's great. Just great. Literally, I can't think of anything better."

"Well, then why don't you tell me your name, sweetheart?" He has a self-assured smile, bordered by uneven dimples.

"Sweetheart? You really just called me sweetheart?" I shout. "You're disgusting."

He ignores my insult. "You came to the party with Margot, right?" He remains calm and collected, clearly ignoring the fire that's visibly building inside me.

"So you remember my cousin's name, but not mine. That adds up," I say. My back is to him, and I start walking away.

"Does your snobby-ass cousin know you go around kissing townies?" he asks, smirking.

"Do your townie girlfriends know you're a classically trained violinist?" I smirk.

He laughs and says, "I like you."

I take a deep breath and try to calm down, to return to normal Avery. "Please stop following me." But he doesn't budge, so I add, "The last thing I need right now is the biggest asshole in Black Mountain following me home. Go back to your bonfire, Jack."

I keep walking and hear him behind me. He picks up the pace until he's close enough to whisper, "Your name is Avery. You were my first kiss too." I turn to see his smarmy grin gone, and he looks sincere for a short moment. "I don't know why I pretended to forget your name. I default to being a dick when I don't know what to say. It's dumb and I'm sorry. I remembered you as soon as you walked up to the bonfire." The smugness is gone. He looks so real and genuine I can actually see the kind violin player I was so smitten with at age thirteen hiding beneath his bad-boy exterior. "Let me make it up to you. Go out with me this week." And the cockiness has officially returned.

I'm completely uninterested in Jack. For one, he's clearly a jerk, and for another, the last thing I need to do is add another worry to my parents' plates.

I'm not the same girl I was a few weeks ago when I actually begged my parents to let me go on a date with Henry Warden. That version of Avery feels a million miles away, and the girl standing in front of Jack couldn't be less interested in boys or dating. But I did come to this party for a reason, and Jack might be the perfect person to help me find OCMC.

"There is absolutely no way I'd ever go out with you, but there is something you can do to make it up to me," I say.

"All right, girl. Whatcha got for me?" His two asymmetrical little dimples start forming on each cheek again.

"I am looking for somebody who I think probably lives in Black Mountain," I explain.

"Do I have competition?" he asks.

"No, I'm looking for a girl," I answer. "Not a girl for me," I clarify anticipating his thought process.

"You've come to the right person. I know plenty of girls," Jack says with annoyingly confident bravado.

"So charming," I say sarcastically.

"That's what the girls think." Jack pulls a pack of cigarettes out of his back pocket. He lights one up and then holds the pack out to me.

"Gross. That'll kill you," I tell him.

"Only the good die young, Avery." Jack's holding the cigarette balanced between his lips.

"Won't argue with you on that," I say as I grab the cigarette, throw it on the ground, and stomp on it. "I need you to pay attention."

"Listening, your honor." Jack stands at attention and gives me a cheeky little salute.

"I'm looking for a girl who has the initials OCMC. If I had to guess I'd say she is a senior, but I don't know for sure. Do you know anybody with a double first name? Or maybe a hyphenated last name who has these initials?"

He tilts his head and seems to be thinking. "Sorry. I can't think of anybody. Guess I can't help you with this, but I still want to make up for being a dick, so you'll have to go out with me."

"I'm not interested in that option," I state firmly. "I really need you to think about this. It's important that I find this girl while I'm in Black Mountain for Christmas break."

"And why's that?"

"She was my brother's girlfriend and I need to give her a message." I try to keep the details minimal until I get a better feel for Jack.

"So, darlin', why don't you ask your brother her name?"

This is when it hits me why Jack is calling me sweetheart and darlin', and trying to get me to go out with him. He doesn't know I'm damaged goods. He thinks I'm still the cute innocent girl he kissed a few summers ago.

Even though I'm holding firm to my no-boyfriend stance, I'd be lying if I said it didn't feel good to have a boy look at me like he is right now. I make a quick decision to tell a little white lie.

"Well, if you must know, my brother is a big deal football player and is at an elite training camp for the winter break. The trainers won't let them have phones. At all. I can't talk to him." I rattle off the first ridiculous explanation that pops into my head, but Jack seems to buy it.

I need to know I can trust him before I tell him what really happened two months ago.

CHAPTER THREE

Two months ago
October 22nd

"Big day today, Avery Jane," my mom greets me as I come down the back stairs to the kitchen. "We need to talk logistics after you eat your cereal." She puts an extra emphasis on the word cereal to drive home the point she disapproves of my diet. Mom is preparing Whit's game day breakfast: a protein shake, oatmeal, and three eggs. As she arranges everything on his plate, she uses a bright pink highlighter and crosses each item off the meal calendar from Whit's personal nutritionist.

I mumble a greeting under my breath, pour myself a bowl of Cheerios (that is as unhealthy as food gets in the Walker household), and plop down on the barstool next to my brother Whit, who is already wearing his Warner Prep Academy football jersey.

Basically, every girl at WPA, and several boys, are in love with Whit. I don't get it, and I'm not saying that because I'm his little sister.

He's large in a way that makes everybody around him look like Fisher-Price Little People. Plus, he has these annoying brown bangs that swoosh over his forehead, and never stay in place. As he eats breakfast he takes a bite, fixes his bangs, takes a bite, fixes his bangs, and I want to dump a bottle of gel on his head.

The ogre stature and bangs don't seem to bother the rest of the female population at WPA.

In my family, my brother Whit is the star. Mostly, I exist as a supporting character in his exciting story. This might sound sad, but it's really not. Anybody who's lived around a leading man like Whit knows being a wallflower requires a whole lot less pressure. I'm genuinely happy living in the shade of Whit's bright light. It's where I'm most comfortable.

"I can't believe it. I really truly can't even wrap my head around it," Mom is mumbling to nobody in particular.

My dad comes down the back stairs, joining the family breakfast.

"Big game today, sport," he says as he slaps my brother on the back. Dad is a mild-mannered accountant at an HR firm. He lives for chances to use corny dad phrases like "big game today, sport."

"It's really not, Dad," Whit replies between slurps of protein shake.

"Of course it is," Mom interjects without missing a beat in her morning buzz-about. She's like a blonde hummingbird in the mornings. "It's your last game as a Warner Prep Warrior. I'm standing over here trying to wrap my head around where all the time went."

"I can help you with the math," I say with a mouth full of Cheerios. "Let's see, ten years of football practices and games, at least six days a week of practice, with two to three hours a day, and—"

"You're going to miss all of this when your brother is gone next year," Mom says as she waves the serving spoon around the room, gesturing to everything I'll apparently miss.

I am sure Mom is right. Whit leaving the house to play college football will be the biggest change of my young life, and I do hate change. I once cried for a week straight after Mom and Dad rearranged the living room furniture.

Frankly, Mom fretted about Whit leaving enough for the whole family. I don't think Whit moving out for college will even feel real to me until he finally chooses one of his Division One offers and signs with a school.

"Everybody needs to chill," Whit says. "It's my last regular-season game. It isn't a big deal. Honestly, I don't even know if Coach will play me much. We are still first seed in the postseason, no matter the outcome. The game literally doesn't matter."

"Coach wouldn't do that to me," Mom shouts across the kitchen. "I can't bear the thought of you not playing in your last game."

"It's not my last game," Whit says, but Mom ignores him.

"Avery, let's talk about this afternoon," Mom orders as she finally takes a seat on a barstool. "I am covering a yoga class for Valerie, so I won't leave the Y until around four-thirty, but when you get home from cross-country practice, if you can heat up the chicken dish thawing in the fridge, we should still have plenty of time to eat and get to the game early enough to save some seats." Whit isn't a normal high school football player. He's a player who requires saving enough seats for his entourage to watch him from the metal bleachers.

"I'm not going to the game with you and Dad," I announce. "I'm going with Riley and some boys. It's a double date."

"Aves, *you* have a date?" Whit asks.

"Yes, jerkwad," I say as I hit him in the back of his messy-hair head.

"Who?" he asks, raising his eyebrows, like who would dare to date the quarterback's kid sister. "Which cross-country goon is the lucky guy?"

"You don't know him. His name is Henry Warden, and he's not on any team. He sits next to me in AP Language," I say, proud to be bucking Walker family norms by fraternizing with a boy who doesn't own a letterman jacket. For good measure, I add, "He's never even been to a football game."

"He goes to Warner Prep and doesn't follow football?" Dad asks suspiciously. The whole reason the Walker family goes to Warner Prep is because of its reputation as a Nashville football powerhouse. When my parents decided Whit was on the path to being a future NFL Hall-of-Famer, they enrolled us in the school that would give

Whit the most visibility to college recruiters. I think most people at WPA assume we are there on some under-the-table illegal football scholarship, but the truth is that our Gran is old-money rich and is footing the tuition.

I started to develop a minor crush on Henry Warden the first time he told me he's never been to a football game. He is the only boy I've ever met at Warner Prep who could care less about who my brother is.

In my three years at WPA, I've learned the opposite sex falls into two categories. The first group is the hermit crabs. They cling on to me with their big pinchers and don't let go. They only talk to me because they want to get closer to Whit, but they could care less about getting to know me. Most of the boys' cross-country team falls into the hermit crab category. The hermit crabs don't notice that I can run circles around them too.

The second group, the cowardly lions, would never have the courage to talk to me in a million years because they are terrified of Whit. This is where my fellow AP classmates typically fall. Henry is an outlier. He's neither a hermit crab nor a cowardly lion, which is why I'm convinced he's perfect for me. Plus, he's cute in a Harry Potter-glasses sort of way.

The only problem is, I don't have any flirting skills. With a school full of crabs and lions, I've never seen the point in honing the art of the flirt. Enter Riley. She's been honing her ability to talk to boys since we were in fourth grade when she'd invite them over only to kick their butts at Mario Kart. She knew I'd never make a move, so she orchestrated the whole double date.

"Henry is picking up me and Riley at her house at six. We're going to meet Riley's date, Ben, at the game. He's in the marching band. And to be extra clear, I'm going to sit with them, instead of y'all."

"I need to think about this," Mom says. "It's Whit's last game."

"Is it his last game?" I ask sarcastically. "You hadn't mentioned it once this morning."

I love Whit. I love supporting Whit's football, but for once can my need to be a normal junior in high school matter to anybody? I don't say any of this out loud, that's not the way it's done in this house. But I do shoot Whit a pleading look.

Mom gets up from her barstool and walks over to the Keurig where Dad is stirring his coffee. They have one of their famous silent conversations using only their eyes. They've been together since they were undergrad athletes at Vanderbilt University, and still act like newlyweds sometimes. It's disgusting.

"Avery, it's not that we don't support you dating. You can date whoever you want, and this Henry sounds lovely. But tonight means a lot to me. We don't know where Whit is going to be playing football next year." Mom points toward the drawer in the kitchen where we keep all of his offers from Division I teams. "If he goes far away, you know, we might not be able to watch all his games as a family like we have all these years."

Mom isn't entirely off base. I usually sit with my parents instead of my friends at Friday night football games. The thing about the student section is nobody really watches the game: they watch each other. Whit could throw a forty-yard pass for a touchdown, and the only thing Riley is going to notice is who wore what.

When I want to really follow the football game, I sit with my parents in their front row seats. I would never even consider sitting in the student section during a big game, especially when it determines our position in the postseason or is against a big rival.

Whit's football career is our family's religion, and big games are the high holidays. You would never go to church and sit away from your family on Christmas Eve or Easter Sunday, so I would never sit away from my parents at a big football game.

But, as Whit has made perfectly clear, this game isn't actually one that matters. "It's kind of a done deal, Mom," I explain. "If one person bails on a double date, the whole thing falls apart."

Whit stands up and walks over to Mom. At six foot three inches, he towers above our petite yogi mother. Whit places his hands on her shoulders. "Mom, let Aves go to the football game with Henry," Whit says. "You don't want to break this poor nerd's heart, do you?"

"Thanks," I mouth silently to Whit. He's an ogre, but he still manages to be a pretty decent big brother. He's the type of big brother who lets me pick the music on the way to school and doesn't leave the toilet seat up in our shared hallway bathroom.

Dad nods in agreement with Whit, sipping his coffee.

"Okay, okay, I get it." Mom relents, looking up at Whit, who stands a full head above her. "When did you get so big and tall?" she asks, looking up at him as though she isn't the one who prepares him his daily protein shakes and manages his weight-lifting chart.

CHAPTER FOUR

I'm relieved to arrive at school in time to look over Riley's calculus notes. Riley is one of the Warner Prep girls who knows how to accessorize her uniform. I wear my blue and green plaid skirt with sensible wedge sneakers and a modest low ponytail. Riley on the other hand puts her signature curly brown hair in a high knot of kinks tied with a kelly-green sequined scrunchie. Riley is like the human equivalent of an ornately wrapped present. The type with a perfectly curled ribbon sitting on top. You know what's inside must be extra special when so much attention has gone into the wrapping.

Riley and I have a lot in common: we live on the same street, we love *Doctor Who*, and our schedules are padded with AP classes. But she's the socialite to my wallflower. While I dread attention, Riley lives for it. Don't let the brightly colored bangles, the flirty makeup, or the glittery Chuck Taylors fool you: she isn't an airhead. In the seventh grade, the whole class took a pre-ACT test, and Riley made a perfect score on the math section. This is why I am completely dependent on her calculus notes and our early morning study sessions.

As I am looking over her notes, she pulls two t-shirts out of her boho sling bag and hands one to me. Riley tie-dyed the shirts using our school colors: blue and green. She also took a pair of scissors to the neckline of the tees, cutting deep vees into the former crew neck.

"I don't think so." I hand the tee back to her. "I'll wear one of Whit's old jerseys."

"Oh my dear Avery, oh my poor confused little Avery." Riley has a mind for math, but also a flair for the dramatic. "This is the type of shirt that will get you to Make-Out Mountain tonight with Henry."

"I am not wearing that thirst-trap shirt." I attempt to hold firm, despite knowing that Riley will probably win this argument. She always does.

"Come on," Riley protests. "It screams Avery is fun. Avery is flirty. Avery has great cleavage. Henry will love it."

"Avery does *not* have great cleavage," I snap back.

"How would anybody know that?" Riley taps her finger on the top button of my uniform button-down, which is tightly clasped.

Before I can champion my case, Caroline Daniel stoops down beside my desk in her cheerleader uniform, exposing her fake tan thighs, and interrupts us. Like the football players, cheerleaders wear their uniforms to school on game days. But unlike the football players, WPA cheerleaders accessorize with jewelry costing as much as my entire wardrobe.

Caroline Daniel is no exception. "Hey, Avery," Caroline says in a falsetto voice. "So do you like know what Whit is doing tonight after the game? Is he going to Mack's house party or like something else?"

"I doubt he's going to a party," I say matter-of-factly. "He usually comes home and ices his arm, and goes to bed early so he can get up for his workout in the morning."

"But is he like hanging with anybody, you know?" Caroline asks without even trying to hide her agenda.

Riley decides to interject. "He's hanging with this divorcee dietician who gives him protein shakes that make him flatulent. Steer clear, sweet Caroline."

"You two are for real hilarious." Caroline has a vocal fry reserved for only classically popular girls.

Riley rolls her eyes and I turn my gaze back to our math notes. This isn't exactly an atypical conversation. Girls throw themselves at Whit all the time. There are clinger boys, and there are definitely clinger girls like Caroline Daniel, who only wants to be my friend to see if I can somehow give her access to Whit.

He could pretty much have his pick of co-eds in the greater Metro-Nashville area, but I honestly don't think he's ever dated any of them. If he has, he's kept it totally secret. But really, when would he even date? His days and meals are preplanned. There isn't exactly a lot of time for anything else.

The only other hobby Whit makes time for besides football is reading old moldy poetry. But I would never betray my brother and tell Caroline Daniel or any of the other clinger girls chasing after him. In fact, not even Riley knows. I'm pretty sure I'm the only person who knows Whit pretends to be reviewing his playbook when he is actually reading *Leaves of Grass* by Walt Whitman for the one-thousandth time.

It's not actually as random as it might sound. When I was ten and Whit was twelve, we were at the flea market at the Nashville Fairgrounds when I spotted a copy of *Leaves of Grass* in a little booth of old books. Being a little kid, I had never even heard of the nineteenth-century poet Walt Whitman, so I picked up the book to show Whit, amazed at the name of the author.

"Look, Whit. Look what I found," I shouted, holding the mint green, tattered book up to my brother. "It says Whit Man on it."

Whit's middle school football team all called him Whit-Man. The entire Warner Middle Prep stadium burst into chants of "Whit-man. Whit-man." at any given moment during a game. I thought my find was utterly hilarious.

"How sweet would that book look on the shelf above your desk, Whit?" Mom asked when she saw it. She handed him a dollar and told us to go back over to the booth and buy it. But what none of us, probably not even Whit, could've predicted is the number of times he would pull that book off the shelf, reading its yellowed pages over and over.

Sometimes when I glance across the hall to his room, and spot him reading *Leaves of Grass*, Whit doesn't try to hide it. This is the best part about being Whit Walker's little sister. I'm the one person he trusts with his secrets. All the little things like Whit thinks Taylor Swift is the best pump-up music, or that he hides Twizzlers in the second drawer of his dresser, and that ladybugs creep him out. He tells me these things because I never look at him and see the NFL logo or mounds of money. Mom, on the other hand, has basically been practicing the face she will make when the camera pans to her at Whit's draft party since he was eight years old.

After a few years of spying on Whit sitting at his desk chair in his bedroom, feet propped on the desk, head buried in *Leaves of Grass*, I finally asked what the deal was with his whole obsession.

"I don't know," Whit mumbled like he didn't fully know the answer. "I guess I like all the exclamation points that Whitman uses. It's like he loved being alive."

"Well, that's kind of a beautiful observation for a dumb jock to make," I replied. Whit picked up a football off his desk and hurled it at the door at the perfect angle to make his bedroom door slam in my face. That's the only time we've ever really talked about his secret affection for Walt Whitman, but I think it's how he escapes and tunes out all the noise around him.

"Where are you going to play college ball, son?" "Think you'll make the All-State MVP again this year, sport?" "I sure hope you get drafted by the Titans one day, champ."

When you get intrusive questions like that everywhere you go, the appeal of shutting your bedroom door and reading a book filled with poems that have nothing to do with sports makes sense.

A few years after we bought the copy of *Leaves of Grass* at the flea market, Whit and I were flipping channels on the couch in our bonus room above the garage when we landed on *Dead Poets Society*. We were in one of those lazy Sunday moods where you need some background noise. I half-watched the movie, laughing at the cheesy end scene where all the boys stand on the desk and recite the Walt Whitman poem, but when I glanced at Whit, he had actual tears rolling down his ogre cheeks.

After we watched *Dead Poets Society*, other poetry books started showing up on his shelf and nightstand: Frost, Thoreau, Lord Byron. The next time I logged onto our shared iTunes account, I saw Whit had purchased *Dead Poets Society*. The movie is so old, it was only $3. I was surprised to see Whit liked it enough to buy it.

Of course, I'd never tell Caroline Daniel, or any other clingers, this intel about Whit.

After Caroline saunters away from my desk, I grab the slutty shirt from Riley's hand and quickly shove it into my backpack. If Whit can't have any fun, at least one Walker should.

Plus, the truth is, I want Henry to see me as more than the quiet girl in AP Language.

Henry is sweet. He isn't nearly as skinny or awkward as Violin Jack, but he's still unassuming enough I can relax around him.

I'm a feminist, and I have the women's march posters in my room to prove it, but I hate that I've never had a boyfriend and I've never really been kissed. Despite what I say to Riley, I fully understand that grazing lips with a violin-playing stranger hardly counts as a kiss.

Do seventeen-year-old girls need boys and make-out sessions to be fully realized people?

Ah, no.

But, if I am being honest, I really, really want those things.

CHAPTER FIVE

When the final bell rings, I change into my shorts and track tee then head to cross-country practice. As I run my laps around the football field track, I keep eyeing the grassy knoll behind the football stadium, also known as Make-Out Mountain. My goal is to slip away from the game and take Henry up the hill tonight. Although it's not technically a mountain by any stretch of the imagination, it is the ultimate spot for Warner Prep make-out seshes. The hill sits in the perfect position where the football stadium lights don't hit it, and it is too dark for any teachers or parents in the stands to see what's going on up there. Usually, my mind is laser-focused on time and form when I run, but today I am caught up in my thoughts about Henry and the promise of a real first kiss, maybe with tongue.

I get home from cross-country and have enough time to shower and blow-dry my hair before the big double date. When I get out of the shower, the house is eerily quiet, like the peaceful calm before a wild storm. Both my parents have already headed out to the football game, so it's me in my room figuring out the perfect look for the game.

I add overalls over the top of the deep-vee shirt to tone it down a little, and then braid my hair until I have two long blonde ropes on either side of my head. I tie blue and green ribbons at the end to finish off the look. I add a flannel shirt around my waist in case the October weather cools down, then I head across the street to Riley's house.

When I knock on the door, Riley's brother Leo lets me in. Leo graduated from Middle Tennessee State University last year, but he moved back into his parents' basement. He works remotely for some software development company, but Riley and I have our theories that he's actually some sort of dark web mob boss. Thankfully, Riley saves me before I have to make small talk with Leo.

"You look great," she shouts as she reaches the front door. Whereas I toned down my spirit shirt with overalls, Riley dialed hers up with fringed shorts.

"You are going to freeze your legs off," I say.

"Being alive right now is all that counts, my dear Avery," Riley retorts, referencing *Doctor Who*. "Now, let's wait on my porch so we don't have to do any parent meet-n-greet bullshit."

Henry arrives shortly after we go out on the porch, and awkwardly, we pile into his used Prius. His car smells like stale Cheetos, and it makes me smile he doesn't have a brand-new fancy car like so many of the other kids at WPA.

When we get to the game, Riley drags us both up the bleachers to find the perfect spot right next to the band where Ben is playing. I'd imagined Henry and I exchanging clever dialogue about our corny AP Language teacher, but this never happens thanks to Riley choosing seats right next to the marching band. The booming brass section played the Warrior fight song over and over causing Henry and I to sit in silence most of the time, exchanging nothing but nervous smiles. It's way too awkward to scream-talk at a person you barely know, and I can't normal-talk over the marching band's noise.

I watch Whit play a little bit, and I am surprised to see him playing full out after he made such a fuss about how this game was no big deal. I wonder if he is doing it to make Mom happy, or if he doesn't know how to turn it off.

Whit has a habit of turning every game into the Super Bowl.

By the beginning of the second quarter, I am mulling over ways to say the phrase, "Shall we go somewhere quieter?" or "I heard the hill is fun and we can talk there," or maybe "Let's make-out."

The football players on the field are a blur of action, my eyes only half focused on watching the game while my brain tries to muster up the perfect play to get Henry over to Make-Out Mountain.

But then the loud beat of the drumline comes to an alarming halt.

The cheerleaders drop their gold pompoms.

I know something must be terribly wrong.

CHAPTER SIX

Freddie from my AP Language class is the first voice I hear, cutting through the eerie stillness of the stadium. "Damn, Avery. I hope your brother's okay." He has both of his hands on top of his head, fingers laced through his hair, wearing an expression of serious concern.

I search for and find the number eight jersey, the number my brother has worn since elementary school. He's flat on his back on the thirty-yard line, not moving. But I'm not nearly as worried as Freddie. When you're the sister of Nashville's superstar high school quarterback, you've sat through enough hours of football practice to know injuries happen. This certainly isn't the first time Whit's been knocked down. I keep watching him lie motionless, convinced he'll move any minute. All the players on both teams have taken a knee to show respect to Whit.

I look down and see my mom and dad standing at the edge of the bleachers, leaning over the railing, trying to hear something Coach is saying on the sidelines.

As Whit continues to lie completely still on the bright green grass, I wish I was with Mom and Dad instead of in the student section. I wish I hadn't made such a fuss this morning about sitting with Henry at the game.

Now that I'm standing watching paramedics surround my brother, it seems comical I actually thought I might end up kissing Henry Warden on Make-Out Mountain tonight.

Even from a distance, I can see my mom's posture growing increasingly tense. Henry looks like he'd rather be anywhere on Earth than on a date with the injured kid's sister.

I turn my gaze away from Henry and notice Riley looks anxious. Her eyebrows are furrowed and her signature smile is gone. It jolts me into reality: the situation is serious. Fueled by adrenaline, my legs carry me down the bleacher steps. I don't bother to say good-bye to Riley or Henry.

By the time I'm on the field, Whit's already on a stretcher and an ambulance has pulled right beside him. It all happens so fast, it feels like I am in an episode of *Friday Night Lights*. Nothing seems real.

Mom is frantic, asking millions of unanswered questions as she hops in the ambulance with Whit. Dad is the calm to Mom's emotional outburst. He's stoic and steady as we jog to the family Yukon through the school parking lot.

Dad starts the car and hits the gas to follow the ambulance. On the anxiety scale, I fall about halfway in between Mom's panic and Dad's stoicism. Our ten-minute car ride to Vanderbilt Medical Center is silent, except for the sound of my jittery foot tapping on the floorboard.

Dad notices my nervous tic and as he parks the car, he turns to catch my attention. "Hey," he says. "You know Whit has a thick skull. I'm not worried, kid."

Dad calmly asks the ER front desk nurse to help us find Whit and Mom. I feel like a little child, quietly trailing behind him. It takes several nurses and questions before we finally make our way through the belly of the hospital to Whit's intake room. Mom greets us at the door, and I can tell the color in her face has returned. She must have good news.

"Whit is slowly regaining consciousness," she says in one go. Both my dad and I exhale in unison, hugging Mom and allowing ourselves to smile. We enter the small sterile room, and I hear Whit answering the doctor's question. His speech is slightly slurred, like

Uncle Rey after too many drinks, but he's able to tell the doctor his name, the year, what city he lives in. All good signs.

Everybody in the room heaps praises on Whit like he is a toddler when he starts to wiggle all ten of his toes. As soon as the intake is done, everything starts moving quickly and they rush him to get CT and MRI scans.

Even though the whole vibe is tense, I let out a giggle when I see my huge ogre of a brother being rolled through the halls of Vanderbilt Children's Hospital. "Aves, are you seriously laughing at me right now?" Whit asks with slurred speech as they wheel him past me. I feel an instant sense of relief he still has the wherewithal to call me out.

"I'm not sorry about it," I say, because really, how can a person watch a behemoth roll past painted teddy bears holding colorful balloons and not find it comical?

Fortunately, they never move us off the pediatric ER floor. After all the tests have been run, the doctor comes to Whit's room to report he has a concussion.

"Unfortunately, with this type of head injury all we can really do is let Whit rest and keep an eye on him," the doctor explains. "We're going to keep him overnight. While he's here he needs to avoid using his eyes. He'll sleep, but we'll wake him to make sure he's all right. We'll reevaluate him tomorrow."

"Will he be ready for the playoffs in two weeks?" Mom asks without hesitation.

"Bonnie," Dad hisses through gritted teeth. "Not the right time."

The doctor rubs the back of his neck like he's heard worse questions from frazzled parents. "Brain injuries are tricky. It's really a wait-and-see game."

CHAPTER SEVEN

It's after midnight when Dad and I leave Whit's room to go grab a snack at the hospital cafeteria. I don't remember the last time I did something when it's been only me and Dad. I know this shouldn't make me happy since the reason we're together is because my brother has a serious head injury. Yet it still feels kind of cozy and nice. The only thing open is Taco Bell, so Dad and I split a chewy ultimate nacho.

"I'll kill you if you tell Mom we ate this," Dad says.

My jaw drops and I point at the sign above us reading "hospital."

"Daaaaaad, you can't make jokes like that here." I laugh. "Come on, man."

We both laugh. When you're this tired and this worried, sometimes your only option is to laugh. Dad steps away from the table to call Gran and update her on the situation, and I finally take my phone out of my overalls pocket.

I have sixteen texts from Riley reporting that things went well with her and Ben the trumpet player, and she asks about Whit. I scroll through all of them and note there are no texts from Henry. I guess watching your date leave a football game to follow an ambulance isn't particularly romantic.

A new text comes through as I'm scrolling:

Riley: Everybody at this party wants to know if Whit will be better by the playoffs.

Riley: Sorry for asking that, the whole marching band made me send it. I know it's rude.

Me: I think he'll be fine. He should live to play another game.
Riley: And how is Avery? You okay?

I don't answer the last one. I'm too tired and feeling too meta as I think about how all I wanted tonight was a nice date with a nice boy and maybe even a nice make-out session. But, thanks to football, I find myself sitting in a hospital cafeteria in the middle of the night, instead of Make-Out Mountain.

By late morning on Saturday, Whit's team of doctors are pleased with his vitals. They release him to go home with strict restrictions about reading or watching screens. When he gets home, he mostly sleeps.

Mom sets an alarm on her phone and whenever it dings, we take turns checking Whit. Doctors' orders. I take a break from my Whit-watch duties to head to cross-country practice in the afternoon.

My mind is all over the place during practice. Our course circles the football field, and every lap makes me feel a little nauseous reliving the memory of last night. It's probably the worst practice of my cross-country career, but all my teammates and coaches are understanding. It's impossible to run a good mile when your mental game is off.

This is why I fell in love with cross-country to begin with. It's the perfect sport for any high school wallflower. The only teenagers who can survive life on the cross-country team are those who don't mind being trapped inside their own thoughts for hours at a time.

Any overachiever who loathes group projects belongs on a cross-country team. Unlike Whit's football career, which depends on somebody to catch the ball he throws, cross-country is all me. My medals depend on my own merit, no offensive line necessary. I imagine this is why the WPA girls' cross-country team is stacked with fellow AP nerds.

The Tennessee Student Athletic Association awards the team across all the sports with the highest average GPA every year. Our team might not have the state championship trophies in the entrance trophy case the football team has, but we have a nice shiny "Academic Cup" displayed for the past five years and counting.

After cross-country practice, I go home, shower, and put on my favorite fleece pajama pants. Much to Riley's chagrin, this is my pretty typical Saturday night. Before I head to bed, I pop my head into Whit's room. When I open the door, I can hear the prep school boys in *Dead Poet's Society* reciting, "Oh captain my captain."

It's hard to feel too sorry for your brother when he is an actual star, worshiped and adored by an entire campus, with girls like Caroline Daniel throwing herself at him. But the truth is I do feel a small, tiny mustard seed of sympathy for him. It'd be sad to feel like you need to hide the things you like.

Riley and I have no problem freely flaunting our weekend *Doctor Who* binges. But I know Whit feels he can't be both a football prodigy and an early American poetry aficionado, so he hides the latter.

When I open his bedroom door a little more, Whit mumbles, "My eyes are closed, Mom. I'm listening to the movie. I'm not breaking any rules, I swear."

"It's just me, dork," I answer back.

"Don't rat me out, Aves," Whit says. "I'm listening to the movie. I'm not looking at the screen. Eyes totally shut. Swear."

"How are you feeling?"

"Bored, but okay. It's not a big deal."

"The entire student section thought you were dead, dude. It's a pretty big deal," I tell him. "Maybe don't lose your helmet next time?"

"Okay, deal, sis."

"G'night, Whit."

"G'night, Aves."

***

I will re-play that conversation in my head nearly every day for the rest of my life. Was there something in his voice I missed? Maybe I should've walked all the way in his room, sat down on his bed, and actually looked him in the eye.

Would I have noticed that Whit was not actually okay?

CHAPTER EIGHT

Sunday, October 24th

My mom buzzes into my room and lifts my blinds while I am still in a deep sleep.

"Rise and shine, favorite daughter," she says in a singsong voice.

I pull the covers over my head and ignore her. Whit is the early riser, not me.

"Come on, Avery. Get up." Mom is rifling through my dresser drawers, pulling clothes out. She finds a pair of black yoga pants and a purple tank top. Once she has the full workout outfit in her hands, she walks over to my bed and leans in to whisper in my ear. "Let's skip church and go to a morning yoga class."

"Let's skip church and sleep in," I groan.

"It will be our little secret. Gran will never know." My gran, Mom's mother, is devout, and was raised by devout Scottish immigrants. She would be pursing her Scottish lips and raising her red Scottish eyebrows if she knew her daughter was skipping church for yoga.

"Mom, do I have to go to yoga?" I ask. "Can't we take one stinkin' day off from treating our bodies like temples?" I bury myself farther into my fluffy white covers.

"I'm going to go do a Whit check-in and when I get back in here, I want to see you up and at 'em, Avery." She flutters out of my room like the blonde hummingbird she is.

I'm about to forsake the warm covers when I hear her scream. It's not like a human scream, it's more like a wounded animal screeching. I fly out of bed, feet not hitting the ground, and run across the hall. My mom is crumpled on the floor in a heap next to Whit's bed.

Whenever I think back to that scream on that Sunday morning, I hear it as a punctuation mark in my life. A semicolon separating the first part of my life story from the rest of my journey.

From the last moment my mom was the person who floats around the kitchen like a hummingbird in the morning. The last day she was the type of mom who spontaneously wakes up her daughter for yoga class and nails a headstand like nobody's business.

I'll never see that mom again.

CHAPTER NINE

Sunday, October 31st

All the lights in our house are turned off and our door is bolted shut to be sure no one tries to trick or treat here. Everybody in Nashville knows this is the house of the famous dead quarterback, so I'm not sure who in their right mind would let their kid actually ring our bell. But I turn off the lights anyway. The last thing we need is to have a cute little boy dressed as a football player begging for candy on our front porch.

Dead Sibling Society Fact #1: When my brother dies the week before Halloween, every time I leave my house to get away from sobbing relatives and casserole dishes, I'll be forced to look at zombies and ghost-themed Halloween decorations. As I jog around the block and contemplate where my brother's soul has gone, I look down and see my neighbor's skeleton decorations clawing their way out of the ground. When I turn the corner and start to think about what death means, there's a giant blow-up grim reaper staring back at me.

Mom, Dad, and I spent last week bouncing from neurologist to neurologist all over Nashville. They all said the same thing. Whit's head injury was a freak accident where the right amount of pressure hit the right spot on his brain at the right angle. At the time the CT and MRIs were taken, the bleeding wasn't detected. When he was released from the hospital, all signs pointed to a full recovery. When he went to bed last Saturday night, he had a massive stroke. The

EMTs arrived at our house in a matter of minutes, but they couldn't revive him. Every doctor we spoke to used the word "anomaly" as if knowing that would make us feel better.

In addition to neurologist visits and taking macabre runs around the block, I also spent the last seven days reading about brains. It's like I believe if I can learn everything a junior high school student can possibly absorb about the workings of the brain, somehow this knowledge can bring my brother back. If I can understand everything about brain trauma, then maybe I can also reverse this whole big misunderstanding and Whit would be back in our house, feet propped on his desk reading poetry. Spoiler: this strategy doesn't work.

I can't stand the thought of going back to Warner Prep or the cross-country team. Going to school is hard enough after my brother died. Going to school at a campus where everyone is acting as though they have lost *their* brother is unbearable.

Everybody, everywhere at school can't stop crying and sobbing about how hard life will be without their precious quarterback. Ninety-nine percent of the kids lighting vigil candles never had a conversation with Whit.

I skip a cross-country meet the next weekend, but the rest of the girls' team draw number eights on their cheeks with blue and green face paint. It all seems so fake. Like performance grief. None of the other WPA runners knew Whit's quirks and depths. How can they claim they're going to miss him when they never knew anything about him?

There will be an earthquake somewhere in the world, or a famine, or some local kid will get cancer, and everybody else will move on to their next tragedy.

But I don't get to move on.

Ever.

And that's the part that hurts the worst about watching everybody else grieve.

So I stay home from school, miss more cross-country meets, and avoid the gaudy candles and vapid tributes.

***

Tuesday, November 3rd

I'm still avoiding school, so I am home to answer the front door when the doorbell rings in the middle of the morning, ten days after Whit's death. A sweaty EMT is standing on my front porch and he looks relieved to see me instead of my parents. He doesn't even bother to ask if they're around.

Dead Sibling Society Fact #2: Grown-ups not related to me trust me with big things, and ask me to do adult status responsibilities because they want to avoid talking to my parents.

"Are you a relative of Whit Walker?" the EMT asks, wiping a little sweat off his forehead.

"I was," I say darkly.

"Right. Uh, my name is Glen Harris. I was one of the EMTs who came to the house when Whit… Well, you know." Glen the sweaty EMT is stammering.

I help him out. "You were here after Whit died."

"Yes. The thing is, well, nobody ever claimed his belongings, so I brought them with me to work today. I thought someone might want them." Glen Harris nervously holds up a Ziploc baggie with a pair of navy sweatpants and Whit's phone. "His phone was in his pocket when we took him in the ambulance."

His phone. Christ. Why hadn't any of us thought about this important piece of him?

I grab the Ziploc bag and profusely thank Glen Harris the EMT.

The phone is dead, much like its former owner. I bring it up to my room and plug Whit's phone into my charger. I'm not exactly sure what I'm hoping for as the phone charges and the home screen lights up, but I am crestfallen when it asks for a passcode.

Whit never used to have a passcode on his phone. Password protection was way too much work for Whit's big hands, and his fingers, which were always so gross and sweaty. I wonder when he added it. What made Whit decide he needed this wall of privacy?

I pick up my own phone, as though I am going to text Whit and ask him why he added a passcode. I do this a lot when I want to tell Whit something. I wanted to get Whit's thoughts on Margot's sluttiness when she showed up to his funeral wearing a skirt that was so short, I got a glimpse of her pink thongs when she bent over to pick up a dropped cocktail napkin. It's like she thought she was going to find a casual hookup at her cousin's funeral.

It takes the exact amount of time for me to reach into my purse and find my phone to remember he is dead. I can't text him. I can't call him. I'll never know if he had a clever remark about Margot's trying to pick up his football pals at his memorial.

I lie in my bed next to the charging phone with warm tears streaking down my temples into my hair. They're the type of tears I have no control over. They start flowing before I fully understand how profoundly sad I am. A familiar "bing" sounds from my nightstand, alerting me my dead brother has received a text message.

Even though I can't get past Whit's passcode, I can still read the first part of the text coming through.

BigGee: Miss you bro. I can't even touch a football right now.

I ponder the sender, and then my mind solves the puzzle. "Big Gee" must be Garrett, the three-hundred-pound left tackle from Whit's team.

Over the next few days, more and more texts appear on Whit's phone. Since most of the texts come from football players and cheerleaders, they're generally short enough to read in their entirety without needing to unlock the phone.

Jayman: I still cry every day, bro.

OCMC: Miss hearing from you.

TessieTess: Love you Whit-man.

Riggins: Hope you're scoring in heaven, dude.

It's kind of cool to learn something new about Whit I never knew. Nobody in his phone is saved with their real name. I have to parse out who each sender is, and some remain a mystery. It's like Whit was channeling his inner poet when he saved his contacts. I send him a text from my phone to see how my name pops up. It's "Aves." My name on his screen breaks my heart into a million pieces.

Will anybody ever call me Aves again?

I know I should tell my mom the EMT delivered these items and I have Whit's phone, but I don't. The oddest things send her back to her bed. Back to a dark place where she can't even look at me, her surviving child.

When the December issue of *Sports Illustrated* arrived in the mail addressed to Whit Walker, Mom curled up in the flowerbed next to the mailbox. She didn't move for over an hour.

Eventually, my dad came out and carried her to bed, where she stayed for days.

I can't risk Whit's phone triggering her, so I keep it charging on my nightstand under a textbook where there is no chance Mom might discover it.

CHAPTER TEN

Monday, November 8th

Riley finally convinces me to come back to school, but it's as unpleasant as I imagined it would be.

Dead Sibling Society Fact #3: Other kids don't know how to talk to me, and avoid me at all costs. Riley is the only person on the whole campus who dares to talk to me. Other people steer clear of the dead kid's sister. On my first day back, when I walk into AP Language, Henry avoids eye contact and keeps his Air Pods in his ears as I approach his desk. I'm about to tap his shoulder, but Riley reads my body language the way only best friends can. She intercepts the tap and ushers me to the other side of the classroom.

"Ignore him," Riley says gently in my ear. "You're too good for him anyway."

***

Our cross-country coach moves practice from the football field track to a run through the Oak Hill neighborhood surrounding WPA. It's a nice gesture, but the introverts who fill the girls' cross-country team have no idea what to do with me. The same ones who drew eights on their cheeks a week ago have nothing to say today. They act like if they run too close to me or my draft, they might catch the dead sibling virus.

My phone is only used to hear from Riley now. None of my class friends or track teammates call or text. It seems they don't know what to say, so they say nothing at all. But when I get home from school after my first day back, I power up Whit's phone and it's an entirely different story. Apparently, talking to me is uncomfortable, but talking to the dead guy is easy.

OCMC: I can't believe it's been two weeks since we last talked.
LilBoo: Miss you extra today.
RideOrDie: We lost the first game of playoffs, none of us were feeling…
TeddyBear: Team isn't the same without you.
Daymaker: I wish I had told you how I felt.

***

Saturday, December 18th

I'm lost in my copy of *This is Your Brain on Music* when my mom calls me downstairs for dinner. She has a full meal set on the table, and she and Dad are waiting for me, looking anxious.

"We need to talk," Mom starts off. Never a good sign.

"We need to decide how to celebrate Christmas," Dad adds.

Dead Sibling Society Fact #4: Holidays are hard. Really, really freaking hard. We skipped Thanksgiving, like we skipped Halloween. Instead of turkey and football, Mom stayed in bed, and Dad disappeared. I sat in the window reading *The Man Who Mistook His Wife for a Hat and Other Clinical Tales* because even though reading about brains hasn't brought Whit back from the dead, it's sparked something inside me I didn't know was there.

Now, it's the second week of December and there is no tree in our front bay window, no lights strung around the oak tree in the yard, and no Christmas teddy bears lined up on the back staircase.

Dad pushes his peas around his plate and keeps talking. "Your mother and I can't bear the thought of being here on Christmas Day without your brother, but we don't want to deny you a holiday."

"The last thing you two should be worrying about is me," I quickly interject because it's honestly how I feel. It's like my sole purpose in life right now is to hold what's left of our family together. The last thing I care about is presents or holiday traditions.

"That's not true," Mom says. "I know we've always had Christmas morning at home, but what if we pack up and go to Huckleberry Cottage when school gets out? We could spend the whole winter break there, and come home after New Year's for a fresh start."

Huckleberry Cottage is my gran's summer home in Black Mountain, North Carolina. I appreciate the idea of getting out of Nashville, but going to Huckleberry Cottage without Whit feels even harder than having Christmas at home without him.

The thought of it makes me want to throw up my pork chop. It's the place where Whit and I went every summer for the first week of June. It was always us, Gran, and our cousin Margot, who's the same grade as Whit. We called it "Cousin Camp," and it was always one of the best weeks of any year. Gran didn't care about Whit's diet or workout schedule. He got to be a kid while we were there. It was his happy place. I can't picture what it would look like without him.

When I don't answer, Mom says, "I know you and your brother usually went in the summer, but we were thinking the mountains would be pretty for Christmas, and the change of scenery would do us all some good."

"I really need to think about it," I tell her. "I've never been there without Whit. It'd be strange. Plus, I'd miss Riley if I was gone for the whole break."

"Aunt Susan, Uncle Rey, and Margot are going. They do Christmas there every year," Mom says. "You wouldn't be alone, you'll have Margot."

The image of Margot's pink thong at Whit's funeral pops into my mind, and I say nothing.

"Take your time deciding, sweetheart," Dad says.

I continue eating my overcooked pork chop and frozen peas, all three of us sitting in painful, tedious silence because we all know the truth of the situation. No matter what we do, Christmas is going to suck and hurt like hell.

When it's been long enough, I ask to be excused from the table and hurry up to my room. I pull Whit's phone out of the drawer. It's become my go-to move. I miss him so much it hurts.

It's been a while since Whit has gotten any texts, but when the phone powers on, a series of little green blurbs light up on his home screen.

OCMC: I don't know why you stopped talking to me.

OCMC: But I miss you so much it hurts.

OCMC: I've thought about driving from Black Mountain to Nashville just to see you.

OCMC: I need to know how you're doing. Did you tell Aves yet?

OCMC: I still love you. So. Fucking. Much.

I drop the phone on the floor like it's an explosive device. My hands are shaking. My heart is pounding so hard I'm worried my parents will be able to hear the thud, thud, thud from downstairs.

Tell Aves what? Tell Aves what?

Who the hell are you, OCMC?

I take a deep breath and pick up the phone to re-read the texts. I try really hard to understand it, but it doesn't make any sense.

Whit was in love?

He had a secret girlfriend.

I think about his prom date last year, Josie Greene. Some rumors were going around about the two of them last summer. But that can't be right. Josie wouldn't need to drive from Black Mountain, and Josie knows why Whit hasn't been calling her. I mean she was at his funeral. This pretty much rules out every girl in Nashville as being OCMC.

Whoever OCMC is, she has no clue Whit is dead.

All I can see are these five texts on the home screen. Fucking passcode. I've got to get into this phone.

***

Learning something new about Whit fills me with a push and pull of grief and delight. Part of me hurts that my brother didn't trust me enough to tell me he was in love. But the other part of me feels like I've unwrapped a surprise Christmas gift. The fact this person who loves Whit thinks he stopped talking to her for no reason takes his death to a whole new level of tragedy. I can picture this mystery girl sitting alone in Black Mountain. She thinks that her football star secret love has ghosted her. Well, I guess he has literally ghosted her.

"I have to fix this, Whit," I say to the phone. "I've got to call OCMC and tell her. I need to know what you were supposed to tell me. Damn it, what is your passcode?" I need the passcode to log in to the phone and get her number. I've already tried his birthday, our address, my birthday, and Mom and Dad's anniversary. I've run out of significant four-digit numbers.

I pick up the phone and call the smartest person I know—Riley.

"You aren't going to believe this," I say when she answers.

"Try me," she says without missing a beat.

"Whit had a secret girlfriend," I whisper.

"Shut up. Shut up. Shut up. That is so juicy," Riley says, adding extra syllables to "juicy."

"It gets crazier," I say. "She lives in Black Mountain and she doesn't even know about his death. She's still texting him, thinking he stopped speaking to her or something."

"You got to tell her, babe," Riley shouts. "That's so beyond sad."

"That's why I need you. Can Leo hack into Whit's phone?" I ask. "It's locked."

"Bring it over first thing tomorrow. We got you," she says.

"Love you, Riley."

"Love you, Avery."

I hang up and feel a little unfamiliar tickle in my chest. Hope? Excitement? I'd nearly forgotten what it feels like to be looking forward to something.

There's a person out there somewhere who loves my brother, and I get to talk to her tomorrow.

I know Whit wouldn't want OCMC living the rest of her life thinking he ditched her for no reason. I'm determined to do my brother one more favor and help this mystery love of his heal.

And selfishly, I need to find out what the heck he was supposed to tell me.

CHAPTER ELEVEN

Sunday, December 19th

The next morning, Riley and her brother Leo plug Whit's phone into Leo's computer. He pulls up a program that will run the phone through every possible number combination until one of them unlocks it. Thirty minutes into the process, I start to lose the tickle of hope, but then out of nowhere the phone pops open and I am looking at a home screen picture of a gorgeous mountain overlook. Whit probably took it in Black Mountain.

Leo hands the phone back and tells me to change the passcode before I get locked out again. I change it to 0501, for Whit's birthday, and then open it back up.

"We're in," Riley says like she is a secret agent in a spy movie. "This is it, Avery. Go ahead and call her and tell her what happened."

"How do I even start that conversation?" I ask. "She's sitting there thinking she's been dumped and I'm going to call and tell her this guy she loves is dead?"

"Maybe text her first. A simple, 'Hi this is Whit's sister, can we talk?'" Riley suggests.

"Good idea."

I open the text stream for OCMC, as I scroll through, almost all the texts are from after Whit's death. It's obvious he must've been deleting their text conversations right after they happened. Why all the secrecy? There are two texts from Whit to OCMC dated October 23rd.

Whit: Sorry I couldn't call you after my game last night. It's a long story, but I haven't been able to leave the house so we can talk. I really was planning to tell Aves yesterday, but then a lot happened. I've been stuck in my room. Not even supposed to be on screens right now.

Riley is reading over my shoulder. "Wow, so not only did he delete their texts, he didn't even want to talk to her at home, where y'all might overhear." She taps her pencil on Leo's desk. "It's so beyond odd, right?"

"I don't think Mom would've let him have a serious girlfriend, He probably hid it so she wouldn't make him break up with her and focus on his game."

There's one more text.

Whit: I'm going to tell Aves tomorrow, and then I'll find a way to call you after. I love you, babe.

It's time-stamped 12:04 a.m., October 24th.

It's the last text Whit ever sent.

"That's the saddest effing thing I've ever read in my life. You gotta text her, Avery." Riley looks at me pleadingly. "Now do exactly as I say," she says, referencing a *Doctor Who* rule.

I read his last text again, and my heart breaks for Whit. My heart breaks for OCMC. But mostly, my heart pounds with anxious curiosity. What was he going to tell me? I take a deep breath, feeling the thudding in my chest, and hand Riley Whit's phone. She quickly types out: *Hi, my name is Avery Walker. I am Whit Walker's sister. Can I give you a call?* Then, she hits send before I can change my mind.

Within seconds of hitting send, we get a bleep back.

"This user has blocked you."

"What the hell, Whit's secret girlfriend?" Riley shouts.

"Shit," I say.

"Fix this, Leo," Riley demands.

"There is literally nothing I can do if the user blocked you." Leo slumps his shoulders at his desk. "You're shit out of luck."

"No, we're not," Riley declares in a singsong voice. "We'll call her from my phone."

It goes straight to the generic message: "The number you have tried is no longer available."

Riley grabs Leo's phone and dials again from his number. Straight to the same message.

"Why wouldn't she want to hear from you?" Riley is now tapping the pencil so furiously I'm surprised it doesn't snap in half. "What a bitch."

"Riley," I protest. "Put yourself in her shoes. This has to be as weird for her as it is for us. I'm sure there's a reason." I'm surprised at the immediate warmth and loyalty I feel toward OCMC. Somebody else out there is missing my brother for real. Not drawing eights on her hands and lighting bogus candles. Even if she doesn't know what happened, she misses him too.

"Sorry," Riley says, and puts a gentle hand on my shoulder.

"The first thing we need to do is figure out why Whit kept this person a secret." My thoughts start to flow so fast that my mouth can barely keep up. "My gut says it was because Whit was scared of Mom, but that doesn't explain why OCMC would be so secretive. Why wouldn't she want to talk to us? She has some secret too. Whatever the secret was, Whit was supposed to tell me that morning."

"Maybe she's in a cult, or a witness protection program." Riley keeps rubbing my shoulder. "Or maybe she's a time traveler?"

"You watch too much sci-fi," I say, while trying to process it all.

"We're sure it couldn't be Josie Greene? Sometimes the most obvious answer is correct," Riley says. "Maybe they were texting metaphorically, or in code. I heard they boned last summer."

"Could you not?" I insist. "Just because Whit is dead doesn't mean I want to think about who he boned. I want to figure out who this girl is and what she knows."

"Shit. This is really dark stuff," Riley says. "You can't live the rest of your life wondering what the heck is going on. If we can't get OCMC on the phone then you have to go to Black Mountain and figure out who this person is and talk to her in person," Riley says, looking me square in the eye.

"How in the world am I going to do that? All I have is four initials and a disconnected phone number." I stare at Whit's phone feeling overwhelmed. "Plus, she clearly doesn't want to be found."

Riley softens her tone. "Whit loved OCMC. You owe it to him. You have to go."

***

For the rest of the day, I think about Riley's advice and her suggestion I track OCMC down in person. Finding her would mean going to Gran's house in Black Mountain for Christmas, which I don't really want to do. But it would also mean I could help out Whit. I could let his secret love know what happened to him, which would relieve them of their belief he cut them off. Riley is right. If I don't do this, I'll wonder every single day for the rest of my life what he was going to tell me the morning he died. I pull out Whit's phone and write down OCMC's phone number. It's an Asheville area code, confirming my theory that OCMC must be a Black Mountain local. I pick up our rarely used house landline and try to call the number one more time. This time the recording says, "The number you are trying to reach has been permanently disconnected."

After I hang up, I head upstairs and stand outside the door of Whit's bedroom. I crack the door like I used to do when he was alive. After a minute, I find myself talking out loud as if he's there.

"I guess I have no choice. I'm going to spend Christmas break at Huckleberry Cottage. I don't know who OCMC is, but I know who you are. If you loved this person, you wouldn't want her hurting, or thinking you disappeared for no reason. I think I can do this for you, Whit."

CHAPTER TWELVE

Tuesday, December 21st

A few days later, Mom, Dad, and I are loaded in the Yukon and driving up the winding hills of the Blue Ridge Mountains to reach Gran's vacation home, Huckleberry Cottage. Gran and Grandpa Tom bought the cottage in Black Mountain, a quaint little town outside of Asheville, decades ago. They chose this spot so they could spend the summers close to the camp where they met.

The story goes that Gran was serving up ice cream scoops at the camp store when she spotted a redheaded lifeguard on the lakeshore. She asked her girlfriend to introduce her and learned the lifeguard was Thomas McConnell. They fell in love and married in a big ceremony with kilts and bagpipes. They had two daughters. My mother is the youngest.

Grandpa Tom made good money as an attorney in the old-money suburb of Weddington outside of Charlotte, and they were able to buy a summer cottage in Black Mountain, next to the camp where they'd met as teenagers. When we were little, he died of a heart attack, and Gran started spending more time at Huckleberry Cottage. She says it's where she feels closest to him.

As we pull into the long gravel driveway of the cottage, Gran, Aunt Susan, and Margot are standing on the porch awaiting our arrival wearing worried expressions. Well, to be clear Gran and Aunt Susan look worried. Margot might be worried, but I wouldn't know because she is looking down at her phone, her perfectly manicured nails tapping away at the screen. I'm clear ChapStick and brown mascara, and Margot is deep red lipstick and fake eyelashes.

"We are so glad you made it," Aunt Susan says as she gives me a big hug. "You and Margot are going to have such a fun Christmas week together. Right, Margot?"

My cousin is wearing high-waisted jeans and a light pink cropped sweater showing off her beautiful caramel skin, an oversize cardigan draping over her shoulders. Anybody else would look like a mom from the 80s in the outfit, but with Margot's shiny black hair cascading down her back, she looks like a Latinx goddess.

"Hey, Avery," Margot says in a vocal fry similar to Caroline Daniel's. Then she holds up her finger to signal she is taking a call. "O M G. Totally, right," I hear her say as she walks to the other side of the wraparound screened-in porch.

"You know, Avery, maybe Margot can introduce you to some kids your age in town," Aunt Susan says, trying to cover for her daughter's poor manners.

Last summer, Whit and I were here for the normal cousin camp week, and Margot stayed at Huckleberry Cottage the entire three months while her parents were in Cuba. "She made a lot of friends in Black Mountain after you and…um…after you and…uh...your brother left."

Dead Sibling Society Fact #5: Nobody will say my brother's name aloud. They think if they say it out loud, it will remind me he's dead. As if I'd forgotten.

"Great, Aunt Susan," I say. "Thanks so much."

What I actually mean is meeting locals in town is my only chance at figuring out who OCMC is. Maybe I'll even run into her since she obviously has a penchant for hanging out with the vacationing crowd at Black Mountain.

***

As we settle in at Huckleberry Cottage, I notice Mom's skin is paler than usual. She walks from room to room as though she's unpacking, but she's not actually accomplishing anything. She looks completely lost.

Mom's relationship with Gran and Aunt Susan has always been tumultuous, but since Whit died it's grown worse. Gran tends to sweep anything uncomfortable under the rug with no further discussion. Having her only grandson die of a freak football accident falls into the "uncomfortable" category.

"She's erasing his life," I overheard my mom saying to Aunt Susan, who defends Gran, as she always does.

It's a mess. But it's not really new. It's always been like this. Gran would've preferred both her daughters marry nice Scottish boys. She couldn't complain when Aunt Susan fell in love with my Uncle Rey, a wealthy lawyer whose family is from Cuba. Rey kept Susan anchored to Weddington and gave Gran a granddaughter with the world's shiniest black hair and golden skin. Her qualms about his heritage vanished.

My mom, on the other hand, took off to Nashville to go to college at Vanderbilt, met a nice middle-class aspiring accountant, and never returned to North Carolina. Except to drop off me and Whit at cousin camp every year.

None of the messy past will be mentioned over Christmas because that's how this family operates. Sweep it under the rug.

Mom isn't the only one looking pale and anxious. As I look around the cottage, part of me wants to steal Dad's car keys and hightail it down the mountain. There's a manger scene set up on the coffee table. My mom owns an identical one Gran gifted her at her bridal shower, twenty years ago. All I can think about is Whit replacing baby Jesus with various Lego characters when we were little: Batman, Han Solo, Dumbledore.

Whit is around every corner, and yet, he isn't. I can picture him sitting in the rocking chair playing cards at the table, or sitting on the counter eating Gran's sugary confections. I peek in the little bedroom off the kitchen, the tiny converted one Whit slept in, and his bed is gone. It's a sitting room now. My heart hurts at the sight of it.

It's the most offensive little sitting room I've ever seen.

I have to get out of here.

I go back out onto the porch to find Margot there. We've never been close, but she is my key to unlocking the OCMC mystery.

"Hey, Margot, can I ask you something?" She looks up from her phone and raises her thick, perfectly arched black eyebrows. "Did Whit ever hang out with you and your friends from Black Mountain?"

She twirls a lock of her shiny black hair and asks with a small lip curl, "My townie friends?"

"You know what I mean."

"Sure. A few times Whit snuck out with me after you and Gran were asleep," Margot answers flippantly.

Another secret Whit kept from me. I hate the secrets, but I'm excited by Margot's response. Maybe she isn't the key to solving the mystery, maybe she already knows about the secret love affair. That thought stings. Why would he let Margot in on his secret and not me?

"Did Whit have like a girlfriend in town? Or any friends at all?"

Margot laughs. "Definitely not."

"How do you know?"

"Whit barely talked to anybody. He kind of skulked around the outside of the group and then left early," Margot explains.

"You're sure he didn't leave with somebody when he left early?"

"Doubt it. Townie girls are skanks. Whit was way too straitlaced for any of them." Margot crosses her arms. "Why do you care so much?"

For a split second, I consider telling Margot all about Whit's text messages from OCMC, but clearly, Whit didn't want her to know, so I keep it to myself. "Are you going to any local parties or anything this week?"

She narrows her eyes like she is thinking hard, and then finally says, "Yes, there's a bonfire party tonight. Are you going to like…ask to come or something?"

"Would you say yes if I did?"

Margot lets out a big dramatic sigh. "You can come, but you have to act cool and you have to let me dress you."

"Deal." I work hard to stay cool on the outside so Margot doesn't rescind the offer, but on the inside I'm excited.

If Whit used to sneak out with Margot, then surely OCMC hangs out with this crowd. I have a feeling inside my gut that this bonfire might lead me to something big.

CHAPTER THIRTEEN

Tuesday night, December 21ˢᵗ

Jack and I are standing in the middle of the path he'd followed me down. He's mumbling "OCMC" to himself, and I can tell he's trying to think about who it may be to help me out with the puzzle.

"Sorry, darlin'." He shrugs. "I honestly don't know any girls with four initials who were dating big-time football players."

"Well, you wouldn't, because I think their relationship was kind of a secret. I don't know why though. It's part of what I want to figure out," I explain. "Do you have any yearbooks? Maybe I can look through them for somebody with those initials?"

"I'm not really the type of dude who signs yearbooks," Jack says. "Yearbook day is for cutting class. I've never bought one."

"Come on. You said you wanted to make it up to me. Surely you know somebody who has a yearbook we could borrow." I look at him pleadingly.

He nods. "Okay, I know what we could do. My grandma works at Black Mountain High School. I could get us in, and we could go to the library and look through some yearbooks."

"Thanks. That's perfect. Let me put your number in my phone," I say with a burst of energy. I might actually be able to solve this with Jack on board.

I start typing in his number and then sheepishly admit, "Okay, I know I gave you a really hard time about the whole name thing, but I don't actually know your last name."

"Jack Crawley." He smiles showing all his teeth and holds out his hand for me to shake.

"Avery Walker," I say and take his hand. But when I go to put him in my phone, I take a page out of Whit's book and type "Violin-Jack." "Would tomorrow after lunch, like one o'clock work to go to the library?"

"Yeah. It's a date." He does a double eyebrow raise, which would be cheesy from anybody else, but is somehow charming.

"Wait a second, back up." I make a stop sign with my palm. "Just friends, okay?"

"Okay. Just friends. No flirting, I promise." He makes an "X" over his heart.

"All right, I'm going to head on home then. Have fun at the bonfire with the ladies." I sound like such a dork.

"See you tomorrow, Avery Walker." Jack lights another cigarette as he walks back toward the bonfire.

***

I don't sleep at all that night. The cottage is built into the side of a hill. The front door is on the top floor, which is where Whit's little makeshift room was. Margot and I occupy the bottom floor. Whit's room was a little porch that Gran and Grandpa walled in. All that was in there was a bed and a small dresser, so Whit spent every evening downstairs with Margot and me. There was no TV, and shoddy WiFi on the bottom floor. We were forced to play games: Yahtzee, an old electronic Jeopardy, and Taboo. Whit was terrible at every single game. "That's another big fat L for Whit Walker," I'd say in a sports announcer's voice every time he lost a round of something.

I lie awake in my bunk bed, curled up in a quilt older than I am, thinking about how I'll never say that sentence out loud again. Why would I? Margot has become patently too cool for cousin jokes, and the only other person who would get it is gone. "That's another big fat L for Whit Walker," I whisper into the air so I can hear it again.

I try to shift my focus to Whit sneaking out the sliding glass door after I'd drifted off to sleep every night like I was some sort of baby who couldn't handle being out with him and Margo.

I think about it until I start to get angry because anger is easier to handle than grief.

At some point, I hear Margot slip inside from her night out at the bonfire and glance at my phone to see it is three am.

I vow to try to sleep, but my brain refuses and continues to flip through a montage of memories of Whit at the cottage.

CHAPTER FOURTEEN

Wednesday, December 22nd

I'm relieved when the sun comes up. I can drink coffee and be free from my nighttime musings and the ever-present grief. After a cold morning run, I spend the morning playing Speed Solitaire with Gran and Aunt Susan on the screened-in porch, and then help Uncle Rey put out a big lunch of yellow egg salad, fresh bread, dill pickles, and Gran's favorite salt and vinegar chips. As I'm finishing up, my phone dings.

Violin-Jack: Can you meet at the school in twenty?

Violin-Jack: This is Jack, btw. The loser who chased you last night.

I'm too excited about the possibility of finding OCMC to try to think of a pithy response, so I get straight to the point.

Me: I don't know where the school is. I'm staying close to the corner of Oakley Road and Virginia Drive, but I don't have a car. Can I walk from here?

Violin-Jack: Yeah, you will walk right past my house. 88 Oakley Road. I'll wait for you.

Me: Cool. See you soon.

I tell my parents, "I'm headed to town. Going to walk around a bit, and find a spot to read. See you around dinner." I absolutely can't tell them where I'm going and why.

When I reach 88 Oakley Road, Jack is sitting at the bottom of stone steps leading up to his house, which sits perched on a small hill.

"You walk really fast," he says as I approach.

I'm a little embarrassed. Is walking fast bad? "I guess I'm excited about doing this. I have something kind of important to tell this girl."

"All right then, follow me." Jack stands and the late afternoon sun catches his dark hair. He kind of reminds me of the tenth Doctor Who, who was more classically good-looking than any one person deserves to be.

We start to walk down the steep slope of Oakley Road toward town when a shiny blue pickup truck pulls up right next to us and stops. "Fancy seeing you here, Jack Crawley," a woman shouts from the driver's window. She's wearing one of those blouses that has tiny bells sewn into the sleeve, which makes a jingly noise as she waves to us. Her hair is silver. Not gray, not white, but true shiny silver, and it is braided into two French braids that flow down to her waist.

"Hey, Della." Jack smiles warmly like he is glad to run into her. "I'm running some errands with my friend."

"Do you plan to introduce me to this beautiful friend of yours?" she asks.

"Della, this is Avery," Jack says. "Avery this is my Grandma, Della."

"I'm pleased to meet you, my dear. Do you go to school with Jack?" she asks. "I wouldn't know. Jack never brings his friends to our house."

"No, ma'am, I'm visiting my grandmother for the holidays. She has a home up the hill called Huckleberry Cottage," I say.

"Ah, yes. I know the place," Della says. "Well, you two be good, and have fun running errands." She winks at Jack, and then rolls up the window.

We continue walking and I have so many questions. Like, why did he tell his grandma we were running errands? Doesn't she work at the school? Shouldn't he have asked her before he borrowed a key or whatever? But I decide to start with "You call your grandma Della?"

"Yep, that's her name."

"I know. But I can't imagine calling my grandma by her first name. I think she would faint," I say. Jack laughs. "She wanted to be called Grandmother, but when my brother was a toddler, he couldn't pronounce a three-syllable name, so it came out Gran," I babble on.

"Well, Della isn't really normal," Jack says, and leaves it at that.

***

When we reach the high school, Jack keeps walking past the big double doors at the main entrance. We round a corner and go to the back of the school building. He stops in front of a cracked window and points. "It's the boys' bathroom by the music wing. I knew the window would be open because the plumbing is shit, and it smells like death in there. They never close it."

"I'm sorry, say that again." I'm praying I've misunderstood something here.

"When a room smells, you prop open a window," Jack says slowly, miming a person opening a window. "I know it's a small opening, but if I can get through, your skinny little hips can get through."

"I thought you said Della worked here." I shake my head. "I figured you'd borrow a key or something." I'm dying to get to the bottom of this OCMC mystery, but not at the risk of my parents receiving a phone call from the Black Mountain sheriff's office.

"Della works in the cafeteria. They don't give cafeteria staff keys, sweetheart." Jack stays planted by the window. "When I said my grandma works here, what I meant was I know how to break in because I've been hanging around this building since I was a little kid."

"Got it. Sorry for the misunderstanding, but I'm not exactly the type of girl who is okay with breaking and entering." I start walking back toward the street.

"Or cigarettes, I'm guessing." Jack pulls his pack out of his back pocket.

"I'm going to head back to my gran's." I'm disappointed today won't be the day I solve the OCMC puzzle, but not so disappointed I'm willing to get arrested for trespassing.

"See, I don't buy this whole innocent little lamb act." Jack takes a drag of the cigarette. "The girl who chewed me out last night was a total badass."

I try hard not to smile but can't hold it back. Nobody has ever called me a badass before. Nobody. Ever.

"Now, Avery Walker, do you want to find the identity of your brother's lady friend or not?" Jack asks like he is some sort of motivational speaker.

He's right. I have no other plan. This might be my only chance to find out who Whit loved, and tell her the sad news so she doesn't have to live her whole life wondering why he disappeared on her. I owe it to him.

"Okay." I nod firmly. "We're doing this."

"All right, girl. Put your foot right here." Jack makes a little cup with his hands, and I hoist myself through the tiny yellowed, dusty window, pulling my sling bag behind me.

"Oh my god, oh my god, oh my god." He wasn't joking about the stench. I yank my t-shirt up over my nose.

Seconds later, Jack is launched through the window and pulls my arm to lead me out of the awful fumes. "Come on. This way through the music room."

I follow him through the empty school, which is all locked up since they're on Christmas break. We cross a room full of chairs, band instruments, and music stands. Jack stops at the piano and effortlessly taps out the *Mission Impossible* theme song. Something about it relaxes me into the adventure. I throw up my hands in the shape of a fake gun and do a little spy maneuver through the room.

"Wait, stop." Jack stops goofing around and looks serious. I hear a jangle of keys coming down the hall. Jack ducks under the piano, and crouches so he is totally hidden from sight of the door. He motions for me over so he can whisper, "That's Old Bo the Janitor. I may've done a little graffiti he's had to clean up over the years."

"And?" I sit down on the piano bench to get closer so I can hear Jack.

"And he hates me. He will definitely kill me, and probably you, if he sees us," Jack hisses.

Sure enough, Old Bo swings open the door of the music room and enters in a huff with a mop and broom in his hands. I look the broom up and down, assessing if it could be used as a murder weapon. I swing my legs around the piano bench so they better conceal Jack who's trying to squeeze his big frame in the tiny space beneath me.

Old Bo spots me at the piano. "Hey, kid, what are you doing here?" he asks in a scratchy voice.

I stay calm and try to channel the girl who was brave and chewed out Jack last night. "I am a friend of Della's. She arranged for me to practice the piano while I'm visiting for Christmas." I gently tap one key. I've never played a note on a piano in my life. The Walker family ecosystem is structured entirely around sports. Music lessons would've never fit into our schedules.

Old Bo seems to decide I'm not a threat. He softens his posture. "I love a kid who is practicing piano instead of stirring up trouble. Maybe you can play something for Old Bo?"

My cheeks flush red. I didn't anticipate his request. I start to think up a lie about stage fright, but before I can open my mouth Jack's fingers slip up from underneath the piano, and a classical tune starts filling the stuffy room. Old Bo does a silly little dance with the broom.

"You're quite talented, youngin.' Who is that you're playing?"

Jack mouths "Beethoven" and I politely answer Old Bo's question. He seems satisfied I'm no threat to the cleanliness of his building, and he leaves the room to let me practice Beethoven in peace.

As soon as we hear his keys jangle away down the hall, Jack pops up like a—forgive me but it's true—jack-in-the-box from beneath the piano and joins me on the bench. He grabs me by the shoulders. "Never ever tell me you're a good girl who doesn't break and enter again. That was total badass how you made up the piano practice thing. Seriously, amazing."

I give him a high five.

"What about you playing the classical piano from underneath me?" I feel high from the excitement of our ruse.

"I guess maybe I'm not a loser townie." He flashes me a charming little smile. "Let's go to the library before Old Bo comes back for another concert."

We move quietly like deer in hunting season through the halls of the building until we reach the dark library. Once we're through the library door, I feel safe talking again. "So you play the violin, guitar, and piano. How'd you get to be such a music savant?"

He shrugs. "I don't know really. Della always wanted me to be a musician, and I like making Della happy so I picked up a few things."

"You're really talented."

He ignores my compliment and says, "Give me your phone."

"Why?"

"Mine is a flip phone, it doesn't have a flashlight."

I pull out my phone from my bag and hand it to him. He uses the flashlight to illuminate the sections of the library until we locate the yearbooks. We each grab a copy from the last three years and hunker down on the floor behind a shelf.

One by one, we scan each page until the Taylors, Madisons, and Chloes start to blend together into a blurry jumble of names and faces. We keep our eye out for double names, but for a Southern town, there are shockingly few girls with double-barreled first names.

"What else do you know about OCMC?" Jack asks after we keep coming up empty. "What does she look like?"

"I've never seen a picture of her," I tell him. "Actually, I don't know much else about her besides her initials, and that she's local."

"This is a weird mission," Jack says. "I think that you might be a little bit of a freak." He smiles, and I can tell this is supposed to be a compliment.

"Keep looking through the yearbooks, please," I say. "Maybe something will jog your memory or you'll see somebody you know."

We both keep turning pages, but that strategy doesn't work. After about an hour, I finally give up. "Well, this was a bust."

Jack lets out a sigh. "Sorry you committed a crime and it turned out to be for nothing."

"Hunh. At least I got to hear some Beethoven," I say. "And outsmart Old Bo, who by the way is straight out of a horror movie, right?"

"I feel pretty confident Old Bo has inspired a large number of Hollywood slasher films."

"Rosemary's Broom?" I blurt out.

Jack comes back with, "Nightmare on Clean Street?"

None of our puns are particularly funny, but we both fall into the type of delirious laughter you can reach only when you are filled with adrenaline from executing a mission through a dark and creepy library.

We decide to sneak out of the building before we push our luck and get caught. As we walk home, he asks, "What's your next move, Walker? Are you still going to keep looking for this OCMC person?"

"Yeah. It's really important to me," I say. "Maybe she goes to a different school?"

"I can start asking around town," he offers.

"You don't have to do that."

"I like playing detective with you, Walker." He rests his arm over my shoulder as we walk.

"Me too, Crawley."

We finish climbing the hill and reach the bottom of the stone stairs leading up to Jack's house. I'm getting ready to say good-bye when Della's voice floats down light and airy from the front porch.

"Avery dear, why don't you join us for some sweet tea and Christmas cookies?" she asks.

"Della, I'm sure Avery needs to get home," Jack shouts without hesitation.

I feel slightly offended he's so ready to ditch me. "I never turn down dessert, Jack."

He looks at his feet and shakes his head back and forth like he is weighing the pros and cons. "The thing is, I love Della, but you need to know, she isn't normal."

She seems perfectly lovely. "It's just sweet tea and cookies."

"All right, all right then, let's do this," he says more to himself than to me.

I follow him up the steps, and as the front porch comes into view, I understand what "not normal" means.

CHAPTER FIFTEEN

The front porch of Jack and Della's home isn't so much a porch as a shrine—to Elvis Presley.

Hanging from the porch eaves are multiple wind chimes with tiny white-suited Elvises dancing in the wind. The doormat is his silhouette, and pillows on the rocking chairs—sequined Elvis. In the corner is a small china hutch stuffed with Elvis figurines. Della is sitting on the porch swing sipping her sweet tea out of a glass with a pelvic-thrusting Elvis caricature etched on it.

She sets down her glass and asks, "Do you like your tea sweet or extra sweet?"

"I'm from Nashville, ma'am. Extra sweet," I say.

Della smiles, which says "I like you" in exactly the same way Jack did last night, then she heads into the house to get my tea and cookies. I take a seat on the porch swing next to Jack and notice the Christmas tree inside the window is adorned in nothing but Elvis-themed ornaments.

I can't avoid mentioning the Elvis shrine, but I can tell Jack feels a little embarrassed, so I try to choose my words carefully. "So, earlier when you said Della always wanted you to be a musician, by musician you meant she wants you to be Elvis?"

"What makes you think Della likes Elvis?" Jack says sarcastically.

"There's got to be a story here." I take my finger and outline the sequined silhouette on the swing pillow.

"Oh there is," Jack sighs, "but it's not my story to tell."

Della returns with an Elvis tray, an Elvis pitcher, and two plastic Elvis cups. She sets them down on the small table in front of the porch swing. "So you want to know what all this is about?" Della asks, motioning toward the open kitchen window. Clearly, she heard Jack and my conversation. I feel a little bit sheepish she overheard, but she isn't wrong.

When you stumble upon an Elvis shrine on a front porch in the Blue Ridge Mountains, you can't help but want to know what the deal is.

"You have any siblings, Avery?" Della asks.

The question feels like needles to the heart. Up until this moment I've mostly been around people who know Whit's story. It occurs to me she's asking a perfectly normal question. One I'll have to learn to answer throughout my life. But not today.

When I hesitate, Jack answers for me. "Avery has an older brother. He's some big shot football star."

"Ah, perfect, then you will understand my story because it too is about a big brother." I lean in to listen and remind myself in this universe, on this porch, I'm a girl with a perfectly alive brother, and there's no need to get teary-eyed or choked up.

"I remember the first time I ever heard Elvis sing." Della looks out at the horizon, and I can tell she's lost in her memory. "I was ten years old and was in the kitchen with my big brother fixing lunch. We had a little radio on top of our pea-green fridge, and all of a sudden this moody voice fills our kitchen singing about a 'Heartbreak Hotel.'"

She pauses. "You know that song?"

I'm not entirely sure if I do, but "yes" feels like the right answer so I nod.

Della continues her story. "My brother was a whole eight years older than me, so we never did have too much in common until that moment. We both were transfixed by the voice on that radio. It was like he was from another world or something. Over the next few years, we bonded over Elvis. We bought all his records, which was normal teenage stuff for the day, but in 1958 is when our story gets a little more interesting."

Della takes a sip of tea. I can tell this is a well-rehearsed tale she doesn't mind telling. And Jack doesn't appear to mind listening. He has a cute little grin on his face. For somebody who defaults to being an asshole, he sure has a soft spot for his grandmother.

Della carries on. "My brother was drafted to the US Army for the Korean War. He was shipped off to Germany, and would you believe the first letter he sent home to his kid sister included a picture of him with him no other than *the king* himself? Just a minute, I'll go get it."

Della heads into the house. "You're awfully nice for patronizing her," Jack says.

Della returns and hands me a framed black-and-white photo of an Army-garbed Elvis Presley standing next to a man who looks a lot like Jack.

"My brother didn't make it back from that war. We hung his photo with Elvis on the wall, and every time I looked at it, it made me feel happy. When I heard an Elvis tune, it was like my whole body was transported back to my childhood kitchen and my brother was still alive. So I started collecting more Elvises, and some more, and well, there you have it," she says while doing a grand gesture to her porch-turned-shrine.

"The reminiscence bump," I say when the story ends.

"What, dear?" she asks.

"The reminiscence bump. It's what neuropsychologists call the phenomenon of how certain songs or artists are stored in our frontal lobe so when you hear them you immediately remember everything about a moment from your youth."

Both Jack and Della are looking at me quizzically. Maybe Della isn't the only one on the porch who isn't normal. I like that she and I share a tragic flaw. We both have dead big brothers. Maybe that's why I liked her so much right away.

I explain myself. "Sorry, I really love reading about the brain. Brains fascinate me."

"In all my years of being an Elvis fanatic, you, dear Avery, are the first person to correctly diagnose me." Della holds up her sweet tea glass. "Cheers to you." She stands and pats Jack on the knee. "You hold on to this one, Jacky." Then she heads into the house.

"We're just friends," I shout after her, but she's already gone, and Jack and I are alone in the Elvis shrine. "I like Della."

"She likes you," he responds with a full dimple grin.

Jack and I make "get to know you" small talk on the porch swing. I learn that he's lived with Della, his dad's mother, since he was little. Neither of his parents were ready for a kid, and when they split from each other, they split from him too. He tells none of this with even a hint of self-pity but instead says he feels lucky to be raised by someone like Della.

He wants to know how a pretty girl like me got into something as nerdy as brain science. I ignore the backhanded compliment and talk about how I want to study sports-related brain trauma in college. He doesn't connect any dots, and my secret about Whit stays secret.

Before I know it, it is pitch black out, and the Elvis decor is lit only by the full moon.

"Oh no." I stand up from the porch swing, where my legs had gradually curled up under my body in a relaxed pose. "I told my family I'd be home for dinner."

"I'll walk you home." Jack stands up with me.

"You really don't have to," I protest, but he's already walking down the stone steps.

The walk back to the cottage is only about ten minutes, but as we mosey up the hill, my lack of sleep catches up with me. I can't even carry a conversation because I am yawning so much.

"Do I bore you?" he asks after about my tenth dramatic yawn in a row.

"No, sorry. I can't sleep at my gran's house," I say between yawns.

"Why not?"

It isn't the right moment to reveal my big lie, plus, I still want his help, and I don't know if he'll be willing to help when he finds out that my whole mission isn't exactly what it seems. I'm not sure how to answer his questions and I stumble over my words. "I've got a lot of memories running through my head all night."

We reach the end of the gravel driveway and stand facing one another. My head only reaches his collarbone. I look up at him as he looks down. "Bad memories, kid?"

"No, the opposite. Really really good memories," I answer.

"I totally get that," he says.

"Really? You don't think it's a little weird to be haunted by happy memories?" I'm curious to hear his thoughts.

He takes a step back and sits on the stone culver at the end of the driveway. He pats the spot next to him and motions for me to sit. "For me, it's Dollywood. Do you know what Dollywood is?"

"Jack Crawley, I'm a Tennessee girl. Of course, I know what Dollywood is."

"Right. Well, it's only about two hours from here, so it's where we always go for reward field trips and stuff. I've purposefully gotten in trouble so I would be kicked off the Dollywood field trip. It's not because I hate Dollywood or anything, it's actually because I love it so much." He looks at me earnestly. "It's the last place I went with my mom and dad, and we had the best day ever. We ate cotton candy and rode every ride, and stayed until the fireworks. Too much happiness around every corner. I can't stand going there anymore."

"You do get it," I say, happy to have someone who really understands, even though the reason stinks. Without thinking, I lean into Jack. Something about him, and his story about Dollywood, makes it seem like he isn't a stranger. I lean in more and he gives me a tight hug, then I stand up. "I'm already really late. I got to go."

"Hang out again tomorrow?" he asks. "I am teaching music lessons all afternoon at a house in town, it's right by the public park. It's the blue house with the big porch. Maybe we can meet up after?"

He teaches music lessons. Slowly, Jack is unraveling all the judgments I made when I saw him at the bonfire draped in girls and cigarette smoke. "I know exactly where it is. That's where we met when we were kids," I tell him. "You were practicing violin in that park."

We make a plan to meet the next afternoon, and I walk back into the cottage with an unexpected little happy bounce in my step.

CHAPTER SIXTEEN

Thursday, December 23rd

The happy bounce only took me so far. I was filled with grief the moment I lay in my bed. Another whole night with zero sleep. In the morning, I get up and eat a big breakfast with the whole family because that's what we always do at Huckleberry Cottage, and I hate change. For the same reason, I play a few rounds of speed solitaire with Gran, even though I can barely keep my eyes open.

Promptly at three p.m., I'm waiting for Jack on the same bench where we met three years ago. I hope it doesn't come across as some sort of nostalgic gesture, but it happens to be the closest bench to the big blue Victorian, which houses Ms. Hattie's Music School. I'm way too tired to stand up, and I'm grateful the bench is still there.

I don't wait long. Jack emerges from the house, guitar case slung over one shoulder as he heads to the bench.

He skips the pleasantries. "Guess what?" But before I can open my mouth to say anything, he states, "The kid I was teaching guitar to, his mom always stays through the whole lesson, which is frickin' annoying, but it worked out for us today." He does a little "huzzah" motion with his fist.

"What?" I try to keep up.

"So the kid attends Hillwood Day School, where all the rich kids go, and his mom is super involved at Black Mountain Country Club," Jack explains.

I stare at Jack blankly not following where he's going with this.

"If OCMC goes to Hillwood Day, or is one of the debutantes at the country club, then Mrs. Sevier would definitely know her." Jack takes a pack of cigarettes out of his back pocket, and then he eyes me, tilts his head, and slowly slides them in.

"What did you tell her?" I'm a little worried about how far my white lie will spread. Jack is one thing, but the whole Black Mountain community is a different thing.

"This is the best part." Jack seems to be bursting at the seams to get his story out. "I told her that somebody left a flute case with the initials OCMC on it at the music school, and we're all stumped who it belongs to, so if she knows anybody—"

"Ooooh, that's clever, Detective Crawley." Jack looks proud of himself. I try to be equally enthusiastic, but it's been two days of no sleep, and it's hard to keep my eyes open.

"I guess cigarettes don't kill brain cells or whatever," Jack says. "I kind of thought you'd be more excited." He sounds disappointed.

"I promise you. Nobody is more excited. I didn't sleep again. You know, the whole happy memories conundrum." I yawn on cue.

"We have to get you some sleep, pal. I can't have my co-detective falling down on the job." He purses his lips like he's thinking. I give him a smile. "I got an idea. Hear me out." I'm beginning to learn he uses his hands when he's excited about something. "Margot sneaks out of your house like every night, so I know it can't be that hard to get out undetected."

I realize as he says this he must've seen Margot, and was probably out with the girls from the bonfire after he left me at the cottage last night. I try not to let this bother me. I mean, who cares if he's hanging out with scantily clad clingy girls?

He keeps going with his idea. "If you try to sleep tonight and you can't, sneak over to my house. My bedroom window opens up to the porch. It's not hard to get in. You'll have a good few hours of sleep and I'll set an alarm to wake you up so you can get home before anybody notices."

"Ugh. That's sweet but I don't think so." I shake my head.

"Come on, your bloodshot eyes are painful to look at. You need to sleep," he says. "You can have the bed, I'll put my sleeping bag on the floor. No funny business. I promise."

"I'll think about it," I say.

Two days of friendship with Jack Crawley and I've already trespassed at a public school, and now here I'm seriously considering sneaking out of Gran's house in the middle of the night.

***

That night, instead of lying awake grieving, I lie there and wonder what Whit would think of my friendship with Jack. On the one hand, he was always the golden boy, but on the other, I now know he was doing all sorts of sneaking around Black Mountain. Maybe he'd be proud to see his little sister bending some rules. That's what is in my head when I look at the clock and see it is 2 a.m. and I am nowhere near falling asleep. So, I text Jack.

Me: Were you serious today?

Violin-Jack: Ab?

Me: Ab me sleeping at your house.

Violin-Jack: Of course. Come over, I'll crack the window.

When I don't say anything back,

Jack adds: If you can break into a school, you can do this. Don't forget, you're a badass.

Me: See you in ten.

It turns out Jack is the owner of the world's comfiest bed, and softest navy-blue comforter. He also maintains an Elvis-free space. As promised, he has a sleeping bag on the floor, and double-checks his alarm to make sure it's set correctly so I can wake up early and return home before sunrise.

I relax in this new space where Whit can't haunt me. "I think I might actually be able to get some sleep," I say.

"No happy memories haunting you?" he asks.

The way he says this makes me worried he might be on to the fact Whit is dead. I try to change the subject with the first thing that pops into my head, triggered by the word "haunt." "Do you believe in ghosts?" I feel my cheeks warm. I must sound like a little girl at a slumber party.

"Hell yeah," he answers immediately. "I watched a documentary on Abraham Lincoln when I was a kid. It talked about how you can see him in the background of all these pictures even after he was dead. I've been convinced he's haunted me ever since."

"What?" I laugh. "Why would a dead president haunt a random kid in Black Mountain, North Carolina?"

"Stop laughing," Jack says, but he's sniggering too. "I don't think I've ever actually said that out loud before. Now that I hear it, yeah, you're right, it's ridiculous."

Something about being in the dark, unable to see who I'm talking to, even though Jack's right there, makes it easier to say things I've never said out loud before.

When I return home in the morning, I'm well rested, and nobody's the wiser about my late-night whereabouts.

So, I do the same thing again the next night. And this time, it's my turn to confess the ridiculous thoughts swirling in my head.

"I am afraid my parents might get divorced," I say out loud on the second night. "We came here to celebrate Christmas and neither of them even bothered to bring a gift for the other." I purposefully omit the fact that my fear stems from a statistic I read on a grief website: ninety percent of marriages end after the death of a child. Jack still doesn't know about Whit. I know I should tell him, but I also know there's a good chance he'll bail like Henry did. Who wants to be with the grieving girl? At best, I'll get sidelong glances filled with pity, and I couldn't stand that. Especially from Jack.

He reaches up from the floor to hold my hand when my voice starts to tremble as I talk about my parents. We forge the type of friendship that's formed in dark places where secrets flow freely. Every time I think about telling him my biggest secret, my mind flashes to Henry. All I can think about is how Henry never even texted or spoke to me again after Whit died. I don't like Jack in a romantic way, like I did Henry, but I can't bear the thought of losing Jack.

CHAPTER SEVENTEEN

Saturday, December 25th

I sneak out of Jack's house an hour early to be extra safe on Christmas. The absolute worst thing would be my parents coming downstairs to check on their only child on Christmas morning, only to discover she has turned into a delinquent who sneaks out at night. I'm extra sure to be tucked back in my bunk bed above Margot long before the sun is up.

Christmas morning is a blur of grief and fake smiles, but having two full nights of sleep definitely makes the whole thing a little less painful. We all go through the motions of opening presents, eating waffles, and drinking hot chocolate. I can tell my parents are as checked out as I am. The "festivities" are made more painful by Gran and Aunt Susan's clan acting like it's a totally normal holiday. As though there is reason to be joyful when the truth is that everything is wrong with a big ogre-size hole on the couch where Whit used to sit.

As I often do, when the weight of Whit's absence becomes unbearable, I sneak away to find comfort in his phone.

When I power it up, a flurry of Christmas texts comes through.

CarOHline: Merry Xmas to my angel

BigGee: miss you man

Nothing from OCMC, but of course there wouldn't be. She blocked his number. I wonder if she's sitting around hoping for a Christmas miracle, waiting for Whit to get in touch with her. A renewed sense of urgency rushes over me. It's already halfway through the winter break and I've made no progress finding her. I have to talk to this girl. She has to know Whit isn't some asshole who ditched her for no reason. And I have to know what he was supposed to tell me before he died.

I check my own phone too while I am away from the family.

Riley: Merry Christmas to the best friend in the world.

Violin-Jack: Merry Christmas. I'm at Della's big family thing tonight. Will I see you tomorrow?

I type out a sweet holiday message to Riley then type furiously to Jack.

Me: Yes. But be ready to work, detective. We leave for home on January 2nd, and I don't want to leave Black Mountain until I can talk to OCMC.

***

The next night, I sneak out to Jack's house. We make lists of all the schools in the area we should search. We both drift off to sleep after several hours on Google mapping high schools and community colleges in case Whit was into an older girl. We're asleep only for a few minutes, when a huge thunderclap booms outside, echoing through the hills. It wakes me up a little bit, but I'm ready to fall right back asleep until Jack sits straight up.

"Avery, Avery, Avery, are you okay?" he shouts.

"Yes, crazy. It's only thunder." A lightning bolt lights up the sky outside of Jack's window, followed quickly by another thunderclap.

"That was really close," he says. His voice holds a weird tremble.

"Wait a second, hold up. Are you scared of storms?" I ask half-joking.

"Of course, I am. Storms are terrifying and dangerous, and terrifying," he says.

"Calm down, you big baby," I tell him.

"Avery, look out that window. Do you see a giant oak tree?" he asks.

"No, I don't see a giant oak tree." Now I'm fully awake, sitting up in the bed.

"That's because a huge storm took out the oak tree that used to be there, and it nearly crashed through my room. So excuse me if I take storm safety seriously." He isn't joking around. Not at all.

"Okay, okay, I'll be serious." I reach down to hold his hand like he did for me when I talked about my parents. When I grab it, it is shaking and sweaty. "You really are scared?" He nods. "Come get on the bed with me."

"Uh-uh, you're closer to the window. Down here is safer."

I roll off the bed and plop down on the floor next to him. "You're okay. It'll pass quickly," I whisper.

Eventually, we fall asleep, and in what seems like no time, I wake before the five a.m. alarm. Jack has one arm slanted across my shoulder and crooked over my head. The alarm goes off, and his eyes pop open, but he doesn't move his arm. We're staring eye to eye. Neither of us says anything, but I break the moment with an uncontrollable giggle. I don't mean to do it, but I can't stop.

"Why in god's name are you laughing?" Jack furrows his brows.

"I can't believe I'm waking up in bed with a boy. Of all the things I thought I'd do this Christmas…" I laugh again.

"Hate to break it to you, Avery, but you're not waking up in bed with a boy." Jack pauses. "You're on the floor."

We both laugh at the absurdity of this little scene. The two of us crammed together in his sleeping bag because he was afraid of a storm. Our laughing subsides, and we lie still, looking at each other for a while.

In that moment, beside him on the floor, staring at his dark eyes, I start to question why it's so important to stay friends. Then I look at the time, remember my mourning family back at the cottage, and leap up to hurry home. It'd be totally inappropriate to date anybody right now, let alone Jack.

That small moment is the only time we've ever come close to blurring the lines of our friendship during one of my sleepovers.

CHAPTER EIGHTEEN

Thursday, December 31st

I'm sitting on our bench outside the music school waiting for Jack to finish his last music lesson of the year. Over the past week, he took my charge to find OCMC seriously. He constantly texted me new ideas for finding leads and prodded me for more details.

"Did you bring a nice dress with you?" he asks as he walks toward me after he comes out of the blue Victorian house.

"I don't know, depends on your definition of nice."

"Nice enough for a New Year's Eve party at Black Mountain Country Club."

I'm surprised. "You got invited to a country club New Year's Eve party?"

"No, definitely not." He winks. "Mrs. Sevier was here yapping on her phone through her spoiled kid's entire guitar lesson. She blabbed all the details of their big soiree tonight." He puts his pinky in the air like he's fancy.

"And she invited you?"

"Invitations are only tiny details, I know when it starts, all we need is a suit and a dress and we'll blend."

"Why would we want to do that?"

"Keep up, Avery. We know OCMC didn't go to Black Mountain High, so maybe she'll be at the party. They wear name tags at these things. I know because I listened to all forty-five minutes of Mrs.

Sevier's phone call with the planning committee." He mimes gabbing into the space between his outstretched thumb and pinkie.

"So we go to the dance and do a few laps around reading name tags?"

"Exactly."

"Okay, let's do it."

"Really? I thought it would take more convincing to get you to crash a fancy party," he says. "I had a whole speech planned and everything."

"I'm growing up. Before you know it, I'll be breaking into the Presbyterian chapel to throw keggers."

"Be still my heart." He clutches his hands over his chest dramatically.

***

When I get home that evening, I head downstairs to the closet Margot and I share. Margot and her family headed home this morning since she couldn't bear the thought of missing her Weddington friends' New Year's Eve party. Actually, I kind of wish she was here so I could borrow something to wear. I rifle through everything I brought with me, and the closest thing to fancy is a long-sleeve cotton dress I imagine Margot would call "provincial." I'm about to text Jack and call the whole mission off when I spot a light blue pile of silky fabric in the corner of the closet. It looks like one of Margot's dresses must've fallen off a hanger, and she missed it when packing up.

I pick it up off the floor and nearly gasp when I lay it out on the bed. I look around the room, half expecting to see a little fairy godmother winking at me. The dress is vintage-looking and perfect. It has a high neckline, which I like, and a little bow around the waist before the skirt flares out.

I shimmy out of my gym shorts and a tank top. "Please fit, please fit, please fit."

I stand in front of the mirror and I'm pleased with what I see. Bonus points, the dress has pockets. For a moment, with the afternoon winter light catching my hair through the window, it creates a shimmery halo and I see a girl who looks like she belongs on the dance floor with someone as handsome as Jack Crawley.

I add some curls to my hair and use some of Margot's makeup she'd left in the bathroom drawer. I brought one small wallet clutch with me, but it only has room for my phone, and I have a sudden impulse to bring along Whit's phone too. What if we see her, and I need proof that I'm who I say I am? I slip Whit's phone in the pocket of the dress and get a boost of confidence, feeling like he is my copilot for the night.

***

The Black Mountain Country Club is a bit outside of town. Jack arrives at the end of Gran's driveway where I made him meet me so I don't have to explain myself to my parents.

When he parks Della's truck, I'm ready to jot around to the passenger side, but he motions for me to stop, and hops out of his seat.

"Hold up. I want to look at you." I do a silly twirl to show off the full skirt of the dress.

"You're stunning," he says in a soft tone.

"Think I make a believable undercover agent, Detective Crawley?"

"Hey. I am being serious. You look remarkable. You know that right?"

I'm caught off guard. It's my first time hearing words like this coming from a boy. I remind myself not to get carried away. There's a reason why Jack and I are only friends. My purpose on Earth right now is to hold my parents together as they grieve and tidy up Whit's unfinished business. Adding a distraction like Jack to the mix would be the wrong move.

I make a point to keep my voice friendly, not flirty. "Look at that suit, sir. Who knew you owned anything more than ripped jeans and t-shirts?"

"It's my funeral suit," he says. "When you come from a big hillbilly family, you go to a lot of funerals." He pretends to brush lint off his shoulder.

"Well, shall we?"

He jogs over to the passenger side of the truck and opens the door for me. "My lady."

Once we are en route to the party, he gives me more details of the plan. "From what I could tell, there'll be a table in the lobby with name tags on it. All we need to do is look like we belong there, head held high, nose turned up, then grab random name tags. Easy."

"What if we grab the name of the person behind us?" I poke a hole in his plan.

"Don't overthink this. Overthinking is how you get caught. Pretend like you know what you're doing, and we'll be fine." He doesn't park in the country club lot because Della's truck doesn't exactly blend with the rest of the cars, and it's probably familiar. Instead, he parks all the way down the street, and we walk up to the club patio from across a golf course.

"You look all sweaty and clammy," he says as we approach the name tag table. "Here, hold my hand and breathe."

The ballroom is decked out in delicate twinkle lights and shiny gold balloon arches. Trays of bubbly champagne flow freely and the attendees look as though they've stepped right off a page of *Southern Living* magazine. I can't deny it's quite a romantic atmosphere, and as we proceed to the name tag table, I remind myself all the reasons I can't let myself fall for a boy like Jack.

"Look, Penelope Parker, I see your tag right there," Jack says in a haughty voice, even though, thankfully, no one is close enough to hear him.

"And you, Mr. Abner Sedfrey." I select a tag for Jack.

"Really? Abner? Touché, Ms. Parker." He says as he accepts the name tag.

We make our way to the dance floor in the ballroom where it appears most of the teenagers are gathered. They all look like they would be right at home at Warner Prep. I can do this. I know how to be in a crowd like this.

"What's your plan, Abner? Do we walk through the crowd or what? How are we doing this?" Overtop of my question a DJ starts playing tunes. The teenagers sway around in a group like a bouncing amoeba.

"We dance, Penelope." Jack holds out his hands. "We dance, and I'll read the name tags in my direction, you read those in yours."

Before I respond to his proposal, his hand is on my waist, and we're swaying to the music. After a few minutes, I ask, "Do you have any leads?"

"No, you?"

"All I've spotted is a table with little cups of fancy banana pudding. You know it's fancy because of how teeny tiny the spoons are. Even if we don't find our girl tonight, if I get my hands on one of those, I'll call the evening a success."

"Stop. Stop talking," Jack says forcefully.

"You don't like tiny desserts?" I asked, offended at the thought.

"Hold me closer." Jack buries his head in my shoulder.

"What's going on?" I hiss.

"I think somebody spotted us."

"Who?" I whip my head around.

"Stop it. Stop being so obvious and hide me." I'm thankful for the dress's high neckline, as Jack's smashes his head into my chest.

"Who am I hiding you from?" I try to stay cool.

"Black suit, hair with too much gel, over by the drinks," he whispers.

"You are literally describing every dude in here," I whisper back.

"Oh shit, oh shit, he definitely sees us." Jack lifts his head and grabs my hand and starts pulling me.

"Why are we so scared of this guy?" I say as I trail behind him.

"See the girl in the pink dress who he has his arm around?"

"Yes."

"I might've hooked up with her. She might be his girlfriend."

"Jack Crawley," I snap.

"We don't have time for that. It's run time," he says. "Go, go, go out that door toward the golf course."

We're both running as fast as we can across the expansive room, and I can see the group of guys in my peripheral vision, ready to chase us. But as soon as we're past the row of arborvitae trees lining the property, they lose interest and go back to whatever they were doing.

We run a little farther until we are far out on the golf course green. Once it's clear we're safe, I collapse on the tightly clipped lawn. Jack collapses beside me. We lie in silence, looking at the clear winter night sky, both trying to catch our breath. After a few minutes, Jack's the one to break the silence.

"You're amazing, Walker. I can't believe how fast you got out of there as soon as I said go. I mean, when we partnered up I had some doubts, but you continually blow all my expectations away. True badass." He holds up his hand for a high five. After I slap my hand on his, he holds on and wraps his fingers around mine.

"Your hands are so cold." He lets go of my hand, takes off his funeral suit jacket, and I sit up enough for him to drape it over my shoulders, then he grabs my hand again, trying to warm it up in his.

"Well, if you think that was badass, wait until you see what is in my pocket." I free my hand from his grip and pull out two teeny-tiny cups of banana pudding. "I grabbed them as we ran by the dessert table."

He brings his fingers to his lips in a chef's kiss and says, "Perfection," as he takes one of the cups.

"I guess it wasn't a total bust. We didn't find OCMC, but at least we have the banana pudding," I say, even though I'm feeling disappointed. Most likely, I'll be leaving this place with no answers.

"About that." Jack suddenly uses a more serious tone than I've ever heard him take. "Can I ask you something?"

I know exactly what he wants to ask. I knew this shoe was bound to drop. I sit up straight, and he follows me up. We're sitting face-to-face.

"Listen, I've had fun the past two weeks playing detective with you, and I haven't said anything, because you're awesome and I like hanging out with you. But I don't get it. Why don't you call Whit? There's something off about this whole OCMC mystery."

Deep down, I know this is the moment to come clean, but I can't do it. I can't lose Jack like I lost Henry. "I told you, his football camp doesn't allow phones."

"Okay. So let's call the place and say there was a terrible accident. They'd put you through to him for an emergency, right?" he asks. "Let's call and say Margot got hit by a logging truck."

"It doesn't work like that."

"They can't hold him captive forever. Can't you wait until he's out of training and then ask who the girl is?" Jack's expression is turning confused and distrustful. He knows I'm lying. Since I'm probably going to lose him anyway, I might as well tell the truth.

"He's not coming home from training." I avoid eye contact. "I haven't been entirely honest with you about the whole OCMC thing. Please don't hate me."

I look up to stare into his deep brown eyes one more time, knowing after I tell him the truth, he'll never look at me as his friend badass Avery again. He'll see me as the broken bird with damaged wings, the same way everybody else sees me.

"Are you the one who is in love with this girl?" He winks.

"No, it's a bit darker than that." I look at my feet and try not to cry.

"Did you murder your brother and now you're trying to track down his lover to make amends?" he jokes.

The tears start rolling fast and salty down my cheeks. This whole Christmas break, I've managed to avoid ugly crying in front of Jack. So much for that.

"Oh shit. He strokes my hair, pushing strands behind my ears, then puts his hands on my cheeks. "Hey, hey. Look at me. It's me. It's okay. Whatever it is, you can tell me."

"It's not okay." I cry harder and he wraps his arms around me. "I'm getting gross snot on your funeral suit."

"I don't care." He holds me tighter.

"Whit had a really bad head injury during a football game this fall. He died. He's been dead for two months."

Jack doesn't say anything. He continues to hold me while I cover his suit jacket in the grossest wet tears and mucus a girl can produce.

"I'm so sorry I didn't tell you. I have his phone, and I have their text messages, and I'm pretty sure OCMC doesn't know Whit died." I tell bits and pieces of the story incoherently, and he listens, probably trying to follow along since I'm all over the place. "I wanted to find her and tell her. I'm sorry I lied. You must think I'm some sort of sociopath."

"You just ran through a country club dance and stuffed your dress pockets with banana pudding. I already thought you were a sociopath."

"You don't hate me?"

"Detective Walker, I could never hate you." He puts his arm back around me.

"Here. I have his phone with me." I pull the cell out of my other pocket, punch in Whit's birthday, and hand it to Jack. "You can look at their text messages."

I watch Jack scrolling through Whit's phone with a serious look on his face. He stops.

"Why didn't you show me this sooner? Look." He holds the phone up and shows me a picture of an overlook with an accompanying text that says:

OCMC: I hiked to our spot today and thought about you.

"That's Graybeard's Trail." He closes out of the text message thread and looks at Whit's locked screen. He points to Whit's wallpaper photo. "That's the overlook at Walker's Knob. It has to mean something."

"Don't you think we should give up? Look at me." I'm a heap of human body fluid and regret.

"No. We gotta go. We have to do the hike." He's still staring at Whit's phone. "This trail was really special to Whit and OCMC. We have to go see why."

"What do you think we will find?"

"I'm not sure, but we'll know it when we see it. Let's go tomorrow afternoon." He jumps to his feet and gives me a hand to help me stand. "Thanks for telling me."

"Thanks for being so nice to me."

"That's what friends do," he says, looking at his phone. "We missed midnight. It's officially the new year."

"Happy new year, friend." I squeeze Jack's hand and suddenly feel that unfamiliar tickle in my chest again. Like a spark of hope mixed with excitement. I don't know what exactly could be waiting on Graybeard's Trail, but for the first time since we broke into the library, I feel like we might actually find OCMC.

It's a new year, and a new chance to connect with this small piece of Whit left here on Earth.

CHAPTER NINETEEN

Saturday, January 1ˢᵗ

Not only is today my big hike with Jack, but it's also my last full day in Black Mountain. Spending all my winter break here seemed like such a long time to be away from home. Now it feels like a drop in the bucket. I can hardly wrap my head around returning to Nashville, Riley, and Warner Prep. I spend the morning with Gran and Mom cooking black-eyed peas for good luck. By the time we are done with our big New Year's Day lunch, I'm ready to stop being so cerebral and try to live in the moment for my last adventure with Jack.

We start on the trail a little after noon. He warns me it isn't easy, and I'm thankful I wore good shoes like he told me to. The first mile is a steep, relentless incline of rocky terrain.

"Whoever OCMC is, she must be tough." I lean against a rock and take a much-needed sip of water. "Honestly, I can't believe Whit did this hike. Coach would've killed him if he knew. He could've twisted an ankle or something."

"Keep moving, darlin'. We're almost to the lookout where OCMC took that picture." Jack points to the trail.

I get back to it and we finally make it to Walker's Knob. We look around for a bit, searching the area for litter or initials carved in a tree. Our search turns up nothing. Apparently Black Mountain locals are respectful of their hometown hiking trails.

We take a seat and look out over the expansive North Carolina hills. It goes forever and makes me feel so small.

After a few minutes of quiet Jack says, "So now that I know the truth about Whit, can you tell me the whole story?

I stare out across the endless winter sky and start the story. I tell Jack about the bears with balloons at the ER and the EMT who returned the phone. About how school got so hard, and why we came to Black Mountain for Christmas. And most importantly, how through the texts with OCMC I found out Whit had something he was going to tell me. The last text he ever sent hinted he would tell me the next day, and he never got the chance.

When I'm finally done talking, Jack leans over me and kisses my forehead with the same gentle way he kissed me when we were kids. I should pull away, but I don't because it feels good to be the one being nurtured instead of doing the nurturing.

"Damn. I can't believe you've been through all that shit. It's not fair."

"It's really not, and now I feel awful I can't solve this last piece of business for Whit." The reality that I'm leaving tomorrow and I failed my mission hits me hard and fast. I stand up and without thinking start to scream into the valley.

"It isn't fair," I scream until my throat feels raw. Then I let out a high-pitched note of anger and grief.

Jack is staring at me intensely. He must think I've lost it. He steps up in line with me at the edge of the overlook, and I expect him to try to calm me down, but instead, he opens his mouth and screams too.

"It's not fucking fair," he shouts, and then adds his own deep bellow into the empty air. We stand side by side screaming at nothing and everything until my throat is dry and my soul is cleansed.

We stop screaming, but there's only a brief split second of quiet before a huge clap of thunder roars, screaming right back at us. I start to laugh at the absurdity of nature mocking our pain, but when I look at Jack, he isn't laughing at all.

"Oh no. He's looking at the dark clouds rolling quickly toward us with terror in his eyes. "Hey, come on. You're okay, follow me." I've gotten a taste of his storm phobia, and start scanning the knob for some sort of shelter. A little way into the woods is a rock overhang with some space underneath.

Bitter cold winter raindrops start falling on us as I take Jack's hand and lead him to the overhang. We crouch close together among a little pile of rocks and I rub his back, reassuring him the storm will pass as quickly as it came upon us.

"This is a little emasculating, Walker." Jack starts to take off his big canvas utility coat. "At least let me give you this so I can reclaim my manhood a little." He wraps it around me.

It's not much longer before the thunder has rolled on and we start to untangle ourselves from under our little nook.

As we step out of the mini-cave, Jack shouts, "Holy shit, Avery. Look."

I think he's seen a new dark cloud and I'm ready to talk him off his phobia ledge when he bends down and picks up a small rock.

"It has WW etched on it." Jack is waving the stone in my face. "Whit Walker."

As much as I would love to match Jack's optimism, I'm not buying the stone. I take it from his hand and turn it the other way and say, "MM, Mickey Mouse."

He takes it back and turns it once more. "WW, Whit Walker."

"Marilyn Monroe," I say, taking it back. "Besides, in the one-in-three-billion chance it actually belonged to Whit, what does it help? We already knew he's been here before. It doesn't tell us anything new." All the hope I felt last night has vanished. I'm so angry I didn't find OCMC, and I'm unable to match Jack's opinion about the initials on the rock.

"It tells us everything." He makes a sweeping motion with his hand. "It tells us Whit wants us to keep looking. It's a sign. We can't stop searching."

"I leave tomorrow," I state the obvious. But as the words leave my mouth, I can hear Riley's voice in my head like a little devil on my shoulder reminding me of one of Doctor Who's rules: Never ignore a coincidence.

"So?" he says. "I'll keep asking around town and you can look through Whit's room at home for clues. You're coming back this summer, right? We will reopen the investigation then." He places both hands on my shoulders. "I'm not going to give up on this, Avery."

I don't say anything, but I slip the small rock in the pocket of Jack's coat, and I plan to keep it in cast it's not a coincidence.

We make our way off Graybeard's Trail and Jack drives me to my street. He stops shy of the cottage, so nobody will notice the big blue truck and the townie driving me home.

I hop out of the truck, walk around to Jack's open window, and toss him his coat. "So this is it, pal. I guess I'll see you next summer."

"What do you mean this is it? Aren't you going to come over tonight after everybody goes to bed?"

"Sorry, we are leaving really early in the morning," I point through the trees at our Yukon parked in the driveway. Dad has it turned around and pointing out, all ready to go home. I can tell Jack's disappointed.

"I... I'm going to miss you, Walker." Jack runs his fingers through his hair. He looks, I don't know…distressed. "Can we keep talking? Can I call you when you're home?"

"Maybe you could email me?" I suggest. I think about my parents. When they're home, I'm constantly hovering, making sure they are okay. They'd notice if I started getting phone calls from a boy. It's so not the right time to introduce that. "My parents have no life right now. There's no way I could talk on the phone without them asking all sorts of questions," I say. I'm hit with a surge of empathy and understanding for Whit, who kept his relationship a secret.

"Are you serious? I can email you? What the hell does that even mean?" Jack spits out. He's getting angry. "Like be your pen pal?"

I think for a minute. "Email is better. You know. You'd be a lot to explain to worried parents. You smoke, you vandalize..." My voice trails off.

"When was the last time you saw me smoke?"

I think for a moment and realize I don't remember the last time I saw him reach in his back jeans pocket for his cigarettes. I shrug.

"I could tell it really bothered you, so I stopped." He looks at the ground.

"Why would you do something like that for me?" I scrunch up my nose the same way Gran does and shake my head. I don't understand.

He opens the door, puts his hands on my waist, and pulls me to him. I turn my face to the ground before he leans in. His lips gently brush my cheek.

"I told you from the start. All I can be right now is friends." I take a step back, out of his embrace.

He pulls the truck door shut, with a loud bang. I can't tell how he's feeling because his head is down, and his expression is hidden in a shadow. I try to find the right words to tell him how much he means to me, but before I can speak, he drives off down the mountain without even a wave good-bye.

***

In the morning, I choose to pretend the whole winter break didn't happen. Jack changed me. And I hate change. I eat oatmeal with berries across the table from Mom and Gran. Since we're leaving right away, they work extra hard to sweep the drama between them under the rug, where, as I mentioned, our family keeps all their emotions, while I work extra hard to sweep away the entire holiday from my memory.

When it is time to hit the road, I carry my paisley Vera Bradley duffle to the Yukon. As I approach the car, I spot a little paper ball tucked under the passenger window. I pull it out and discover it's actually a piece of notebook paper wrapped around a rock, held together with a rubber band. I unfold the piece of paper and read the note.

Avery,

I defaulted to being an asshole again, but you make me want to be a better person. I promise to be the best damn pen pal anybody's ever had. Check your email.

Yours, Jack

I examine the rock that the note was wrapped around. It's the WW rock that I had tucked into Jack's coat pocket yesterday.

I clutch the note in one hand and the WW rock in the other.

CHAPTER TWENTY

Wednesday, January 5ᵗʰ

I feel like I'm starring in a low-budget commercial for a teen crisis hotline featuring a montage of angsty clichés. Some days, I grieve Whit. Other days I grieve OCMC: the fact she exists and I failed to find her. I hate that Whit needed to tell me something, and I hate she's walking around thinking Whit is some sort of a jerk when that couldn't be further from the truth.

Dead Sibling Society Fact #6: I'm surprised how quickly I've forgotten my brother's flaws, which used to drive me crazy daily and how instead I canonize him.

It's the first class of the first day back from winter break, and I'm already dreading the whole damn semester. I have AP Chemistry first period and Ms. Macabee doesn't waste a minute with the normal first day after break bullshit. She gets right to the point and announces she'll be assigning lab partners for the semester in alphabetical order. I scan the room looking for who are the fellow "Ws" and my gaze lands on none other than Henry Warden. He still hasn't spoken to me since the night White got hurt, and honestly, I can't think of a single person at Warner Prep I'd hate to be paired with more than Henry. I say a silent prayer the lab work will be minimal, but Ms. Macabee's voice cuts through my plea as though she can hear my thoughts.

"Most of your second semester grade will be based on partner work. If you want an A in this class, you're going to have to get to know your lab partner well. Go ahead and take ten minutes to exchange contact information and start getting to know your partner."

I sit still at my desk and watch Henry Warden s-l-o-w-l-y scoot his chair across the floor to my lab table. Not only did he bail on me when he should've been supportive, but knowing he's going to count on us getting an A is way more pressure than I need right now. Henry's on track to be the valedictorian of our class. As long as he doesn't wind up with a lab partner who screws up his GPA.

I can hear the second hand on the classroom wall clock ticking slowly above the door as Henry and I stare at each other, waiting to see who'll be the first to say something.

"So, I think you already have my number, but here's my email address." I write my school-issued contact info on a corner of notebook paper and rip it out, avoiding any skin-to-skin contact as I hand it to Henry.

"Thanks," he says and adjusts his Harry Potter frames. "This whole lab partner thing feels like a lot of pressure."

"Pressure for you?" I laugh uneasily. "Imagine the pressure on me. I don't want to be the girl who makes you get your first ever B."

"Oh, come on, Avery. You're like the smartest girl in our class," he says, relaxing a little and seeming slightly less afraid of being partnered with the dead kid's sister.

"You realize that's a pretty misogynistic compliment," I retort.

"So sorry. I didn't mean it like that, I..." he stutters all over himself, and tenses up again. He looks panicked to change the subject. "You're reading *The League of Denial?*" He points to the black book spine under my chemistry notebook. It's a book detailing traumatic brain injuries in the NFL.

I nod.

Henry looks pleased, like he finally thought of something appropriate to say to terribly scary Avery Walker.

"You ever thought about going to Boston University?" he asks. "I did some college tours in Boston over Christmas break, and BU has some really cutting-edge research in sports-related brain injuries."

"Yeah," I mutter. "I've heard that before. BU is kind of at the top of my college list." I'm not being polite. This is completely true. The more I learn about neuroscience, the more I want to help solve the problem of brain injuries in high school athletes. Since I couldn't save Whit, maybe I can save somebody else's brother.

"Really?" Henry says. "My top school is in Boston too, well, Cambridge actually." These are the types of things I'd hoped we'd talk about on our date. I take an internal sigh and think of the alternate timeline where our date isn't cut short, and Henry and I discover we have these things in common.

"So did you like Boston when you visited?"

"It's a lot colder than Nashville, but still pretty awesome," he says. "My brother has lived there for a while." I remember Henry and I have something else besides our nerdiness in common: superstar older brothers. But Henry's brother is the political academia type who landed at Harvard with a ten-year plan to become a junior senator. And Henry's brother is alive.

Maybe being partnered with Henry won't be so bad. I still don't forgive him for ignoring me after our date was cut short, but I am starting to remember the small things that made me develop my little crush last fall.

He reminds me of a miniature professor. Like one of those tiny shrunken sponges we used to get in our Christmas stocking. Add water to the dinosaur or unicorn, and it grows into full size. I imagine when Henry breaks free of this jock-riddled school he'll grow into an Indiana Jones-stye professor.

Ms. Macabee calls out our ten minutes are up, and dives into a lecture on chemical bonds.

***

After school starts, I get into the habit of checking my email every day at lunch to see what my pen pal has to say. My inbox is full of fun anecdotes, like Jack pranking Old Bo. Jack writes in great detail about putting a fake ad on Craigslist advertising baby goats, pre-trained for hipster goat-yoga. He listed Bo's number as the contact. I re-read that email and laugh out loud, picturing Ole' Bo fielding calls about goat-yoga. Jack ends every email with some version of the same question: Found any clues in Whit's room, detective?

I ignore the question, because the truth is I haven't been able to make it past the doorframe. Aunt Susan went in Whit's room to pick out a suit for his funeral, and as far as I know, that's the last time anybody's been in there.

It's a time capsule I'm not yet ready to dig up.

***

The winter is the coldest I can remember, and Riley's mom knits both of us ridiculously long rainbow scarves, like Doctor Who's. When I go over to Riley's house to get the scarf, I try it on and ask Riley to snap a picture of me all wrapped up in my colorful scarf to email to Jack.

"Wow, you are so in love with this boy," she says.

"I'm really not," I state with emphasis. "I appreciate he cares about helping me with OCMC. He's a good friend."

Riley hands me her phone and asks if I'll return the favor and snap a picture of her. "Don't you want to know who my picture is for?" she asks as she poses with pouty lips.

"Is it for Ben the trumpet player?"

"Come on, Avery. You've been so busy with your pen pal you're not keeping up. Ben is old news." Riley hands me her phone so I can see a picture of her new guy.

"Is that Will Peterson from down the street?" I ask. We used to play with Will all the time when we were in elementary school, but

Riley and I ended up at Warner Prep and Will ended up at our neighborhood public school so we drifted apart.

"Sure is." Riley smiles big and looks at the picture with doe eyes. "I was bored while you were gone for winter break. Will and I reconnected." Riley fills me in on all the juicy details that I've missed.

"I'm so happy for you." I give her a big bear hug.

"I want to see you happy too," she says. "If I come with you, would you go in Whit's room? I agree with Violin Jack. I think there could be clues in there."

"I don't know." I sigh.

"Don't you *need* to know what he was planning to tell you?" Riley asks. "I'll hold your hand the whole time."

I shake my head, and Riley recites a Doctor Who rule: "Never run when you are scared."

CHAPTER TWENTY-ONE

Friday, January 21ˢᵗ

As promised, Riley holds my hand tight as we enter Whit's room. It smells stale, like old food and gym socks. I walk across the dusty carpet to his desk and run my fingers along all his favorite poetry books. Riley follows closely behind.

I sit in his desk chair and start to open each drawer one by one. It feels all wrong. I'd rather die than have Whit go through my drawers. "I can't do this," I mutter, and stand up before Riley can talk me out of it.

I cross the hall to my room and collapse on my bed, but Riley doesn't follow. I bury my head in my pillow and start mentally drafting an email to Jack.

A few minutes later, Riley interrupts my flow. She tosses some glossy brochures in my direction. I sit up and look closer. They're the type of promotional materials college admissions reps pass out at the fair at the mall. Why would Whit ever go to a college fair? Colleges were after him, not the other way around. I flip through the brochures.

Oberlin.

Wesleyan.

Sewanee.

None of these colleges even have football teams.

"Do you think he wanted to quit football?" I whisper. It seems impossible. "I mean football was his entire life. Maybe he took these to be polite or something?"

"Avery, think about it. If he was hiding he was in love with somebody, he could've been hiding this too." I can tell Riley is thinking hard because she is twirling a spiral of her hair. "Maybe this is what he was going to tell you. He would've needed a lot of moral support if he was going to break this shit to your parents."

I don't know what to say. My hand is shaking uncontrollably and Riley grabs it. This is the most painful stab of grief I have felt yet. There was so much to Whit that I'll never get to know. Riley registers the pain on my face and doesn't say anything. We lie in bed holding hands.

It's dark out when Riley stands up. "I need to go, but I'm going to put these right here." She shoves the brochures under my mattress. "We can leave them there until you're ready."

***

The next week, I meet Henry in the library during study hall so we can review our chemical bonds notes together. We spread out our stuff on a square table and I am ready to dive into chemistry when Henry takes me by surprise.

"I owe you an apology," Henry says.

I look at him and wave my hand in the air indicating "Go on."

"I'm really sorry I didn't call or text you after our date last fall. It was pretty uncool. I didn't know what to say, not that that's an excuse."

"I get it." Even though it's not how I felt last fall. "It wasn't exactly an ideal first date."

"Even before you left, there was so much I wanted to say, but the band was so loud. I knew I'd have to yell, and I was worried I would wind up spraying spit all over you while I tried to talk over everything."

I laugh and then remember we are in the middle of the library. I lower my voice. "Me too, Henry. Seriously, I was thinking the same exact thing while we were at the game."

"So should we blame the marching band for our failed first date?" Henry asks.

"Well, that and my brother's whole little fatal injury thing."

His cheeks flush red, and I can see I've made him uncomfortable, but I don't feel bad. Death is uncomfortable. Being friends with a grieving sister is uncomfortable.

"Listen, if you're going to be my lab partner, you should know my sense of humor has gotten kinda dark in the last few months."

"I can do dark humor," he says and nods like he's considering it. "What do you do with a dead chemist?"

"Um, I don't know."

"You Barium," Henry says then laughs at his own chemistry pun.

"That was pretty good, Warden," I say. "I see why you're Harvard material." I take my pencil and point it at the word "Harvard" scrolled across Henry's crimson hoodie. We smile at each other, holding eye contact for a fleeting second before turning our heads back to our chemistry notes.

***

Jack and I write to each other every day. He agrees with Riley's theory that Whit was going to tell me he planned to quit football. Jack also fills me in on his new job as a barista at the Blue Ridge Roast. He misses teaching music, but likes the coffee shop manager, Andy, who went to a fancy-pants private school in Asheville. Jack thinks Andy might be able to help expand our search for OCMC.

My emails to Jack are filled with all the small details of my days. I tell him everything about Riley's budding romance with Will, and the latest brain books I'm reading. For obvious reasons, I omit Henry from my stories even though I'm spending most of my free time with him. It feels wrong to be developing feelings for Henry all over again when I made it clear to Jack we couldn't be together because having a boyfriend would freak my parents out. But the truth is, me having a boyfriend wouldn't actually bother my parents. Having a boyfriend like Henry would thrill them.

It's having a boyfriend like Jack I fear might send them over the edge of parental worry.

**

Dead Sibling Society Fact #7: Formerly madly-in-love parents will fight a lot and play the blame game every single day. From my perch on our back staircase, I overhear conversations in the kitchen, featuring gems like

"If only you hadn't pushed him so hard at football, Bonnie."

"How can you be back at work like life is normal, Charles?"

"How are we supposed to keep going like this?"

After several weeks of constant arguing, my parents sit me down for pork chops and peas, the classic Walker family meal for big family talks. I tremble at the table, bracing myself to hear the words "separation" or "divorce."

Dad skips the small talk and gets straight to the point. "As you might have noticed, your mother and I are going through a rough patch right now."

"I've sorta noticed," I say, and bite my lip from adding "duh" onto the end of the sentence.

"We have a decision for you to make, sweetheart," Mom says. I choke back tears and imagine my mom is about to ask who I want to live with when they split, but she doesn't. "How would you feel about spending the entire summer with Gran in Black Mountain while your dad and I work on things between us?"

"Oh, of course," I say without any hesitation. "I would love that." They both look surprised at how quickly I answer the question, and I have to remind myself they're completely in the dark about my mission to find OCMC and how great a whole summer of detective work will be.

"What about cross-country?" Dad asks. "You'd have to miss summer training. Would that be okay?"

It's amazing my dad could possibly still think it's healthy for a teenager's life to be centered around a sport, but there's no chance I'll say this out loud. When Whit was alive, I lived to be the supportive little sister, now my role is the supportive daughter, holding this bruised little clan together.

"Black Mountain would be a great place to train this summer," I answer. "The altitude would be a challenge. By the time I get back to six hundred feet above sea level in Nashville, I'll be ready for anything."

"Great news," they say nearly in unison, giving me a glimmer of hope for their future together.

"What about Riley?" Mom asks. "I know you would miss her a lot. You two have such sweet summer traditions." I smile thinking about our late-night walks to buy half-price milkshakes at Sonic, but I know Riley will be busy doing late-night stuff with Will. The truth is, if there were a friend I was going to miss terribly, it would probably be Henry.

"I'll miss my friends, but I really want to go." This isn't even a choice. It's an easy yes. Nothing in Nashville is as important to me as finding OCMC.

As soon as I leave the dinner table, I run to my room, skipping every other step on the back stairs to get to my computer to email Jack the good news.

CHAPTER TWENTY-TWO

Friday, April 15th

Henry and I are constant study-buddies. It's good to have a friend to hang out with, especially since Riley has been so busy with Will, and none of my old running buddies are exactly beating down my door to work out together. Today, Henry and I are in the library during study hall reviewing for our test on ionic solids when he starts acting even more awkward than normal.

Our AP study guides are open and spread out all over the table. We're filling in answers quietly, but Henry keeps tapping his pencil and glancing over at me like he wants to say something. The edges of his mouth keep curling up, but nothing comes out, until he finally squeaks, "I think the answer to the fourth question is on page one-sixty-two."

"I actually already know the answer to that one," I say, glancing down at my notes. "It's a systematic periodic three-D ray."

"Why don't you check page one-sixty-two to be sure." Henry hands me the heavy chemistry textbook, already open to the correct page.

"I'm sure," I say even more confidently, pushing the book back over to his side of the table.

"But…check the page." He scoots the book back to me.

"Why are you being weird, Warden?" I lean back in my chair and scrunch up my face.

"Can you look at page one-sixty-two, Avery?" He's so insistent about page 162 he's starting to get little beads of sweat at his hairline.

Even though I'm certain that my answer is correct—I took good notes on the structure of ionic solids—I humor him and turn to page 162. There in the bottom corner, scribbled in pencil, it says, "Will you go to prom with me?"

A little smile spreads slowly across my lips. "You are never going to get into Harvard if you vandalize school property," I say. "But I'll go to prom with you anyway."

Henry's smile is wider than mine. "I was really nervous to ask. I'm glad you said yes. It can be like a first-date do-over."

"I'd like that," I say, but I look down to my notes quickly, so my face doesn't give away how I actually feel. It's nothing personal. In a perfect world, I would love nothing more than to ride in a limo, dance to cheesy music, and have a first-date do-over with Henry. But the reality is, like Christmas, prom will be hard. Really freaking hard. Whit should be there, probably being crowned prom king, but he won't be, and not even a promposal from your former crush can take that pain away.

***

Prom falls on May 1st, which would've been Whit's nineteenth birthday. He was older than most of his class because, of course, my parents held him back for sports. I know he would've liked the pomp and circumstance of being the birthday boy at prom, and I wonder if he was here if he would have gotten up the courage to ask OCMC to come to town.

Why didn't you want us all to know this girl, Whit?

Last year he took Josie Greene, captain of the cheerleaders. They looked perfect together posing for pictures around the Greenes' oasis-like swimming pool. Was Whit actually thinking about OCMC as he smiled for those pictures? Was that why he was home from prom before midnight? I always presumed he came home early because he cared so much about his morning workouts. Maybe he didn't care as much about football as we all thought.

Gran comes to town the week before prom and takes me to pick out a dress. We go to Glitz Bridal and she splurges on a flowy light pink chiffon gown. She likes it because the fabric "looks expensive," and I like it because it's an unobtrusive color and it has hidden little pockets for my phone. After New Year's Eve, I'll never attend another formal event in my life without dress pockets. It's a total game changer.

Mom braids my hair into two tight French braids and twists them together to form the illusion of a braided crown around my head. I love it and I love seeing Mom care about things she used to obsess over. Silly things like fixing my hair. Dad follows me around with his camera, snapping pictures of my hair and makeup. The whole scene feels so typical and normal, it nearly makes me cry happy tears.

After enough pictures have been taken to satisfy Mom and Riley's mom, Henry, Riley, Will, and I pile into Will's vintage red Mustang. The last time I hung out with Will we were ten years old and obsessed with Pokémon cards. I can tell he has grown into the perfect match for Riley. He is like a human golden retriever, and Riley is loving the nonstop attention and affection. We go to the Mercantile on Broadway for dinner, and then we head to the downtown walking bridge to take more photo snapping.

Is it even prom if your social media isn't overflowing with staged shots?

Henry and I mostly do silly pictures, like the awkward prom pose with his arms around me from behind, 1980s style. Riley and Will, on the other hand, suck face in every shot, and Henry and I can't look each other in the eye while they make-out for the camera.

Every moment their lips are locked, it feels like the pressure increases for what will happen between Henry and me at the end of the night.

When you go to a school like Warner Prep Academy, there's no reason to rent a hotel ballroom for your prom. Our cafeteria can best be described as Hogwarts, but with anchored candelabras instead of floating ones. Move the tables out, and you have the world's most charming and romantic space for a high school dance.

The party is in full swing when our crew walks into the beautifully lit cafeteria. The twinkle lights remind me of the Black Mountain Country Club, but I try to push the memory out of my mind and focus on the present.

We dance in a group, and I'm surprised to see Henry is less timid than I would've guessed. He puts his hands on my waist and actually has some legit moves. I'm lost in the moment, enjoying this new side of him, when my dress pocket starts vibrating.

Dead Sibling Society Fact #8: When my phone rings at an unexpected time, I'm assuming it's because somebody I love died.

I pull my phone out and see Jack's name. In all the months of emailing, he's never called me. I know I shouldn't leave prom to talk to Jack, especially since this is supposed to be my and Henry's "do-over" date. Jack is breaking our rules, so I hit "decline" and make a mental note to email him as soon as I am home.

Dead Sibling Society Fact #8.5: If somebody calls me three times in a row, I will no longer assume somebody died, I will be one hundred percent certain that's the only possible explanation.

When "Violin-Jack" pops up on my screen for the third time, I leave my merry troupe of dancing friends and step out into a dark school hallway. I lean against a locker, to see if he will call a fourth time. He does.

"Hello," I answer.

"Thank god, you answered." Jack's voice sounds both familiar and strange at the same time.

"What's the matter?"

"It's Whit's birthday, and I've been thinking about you all day. You didn't email me back and I was worried."

"How'd you know it was Whit's birthday?" I mentally scan my recent emails, but I'm sure I hadn't mentioned it, or prom, or Henry.

"It was the passcode for his phone," Jack says. "I know I wasn't supposed to call, but you didn't email, and I needed to know you're okay."

"I'm okay," I answer. "I mean it. I really am."

"It's really good to hear your voice," he says. "Sometimes when I read your emails I start to wonder if I imagined you."

"I know what you mean. It's good to hear your voice too." I am wearing a perfect dress on a date with a nice guy, and yet here I am, standing outside the dance, leaning against a locker, talking to Jack. A group of rowdy football boys in tuxes pass by me and shout, "Hey, little Walker."

"Are you out somewhere?" Jack asks, sounding surprised when he hears the background noise.

"Yeah, I'm at prom, actually."

"Are you with Riley?"

"Yes," I answer, which technically was a lie.

"Okay, tell her I said hi."

"I will."

"Avery?"

"Yeah?"

"I'm really excited to see you in a few weeks."

"Me too, Jack."

I hold the phone against my chest for a few minutes, getting myself together before I go back into the dance, but the effort is in vain. The way I'm feeling about Henry changed with one phone call. If I'm honest, the way I've felt about Henry all semester had changed since last year.

When I make my way back to my friends, I have only one thing on my mind.

***

When the night is over, Will drives us home, and Henry hops out of the Mustang to walk me to the door. I might be naive and inexperienced, but I know what's expected after prom. I'm pretty sure I don't want to kiss Henry, but he expects it. I'm entirely certain I don't want to be thinking about Jack if I do, and he's the only thing on my mind.

I give Henry a little side hug and bolt through the door before anything else can happen.

CHAPTER TWENTY-THREE

Saturday, May 28th

The last school bell of junior year rang less than twelve hours ago and Mom and I are already on the road heading to North Carolina. Exactly like Henry didn't know what to say after Whit died last fall, he was equally clueless about how to act after I didn't kiss him on prom night. After our last chemistry lab assignment was due, he avoided me, exactly like last fall.

When we arrive at the cottage, Gran has a big lunch spread out for us. I sit down at the table on the back screened porch and eat my ham and cheese sandwich as fast as I can. My foot's tapping like a rabbit's against the side of the table until I find an opening to say, "I'm going to go for a run. I'll be back soon." Neither Gran nor Mom seems to notice I'm wearing cut-off jean shorts and a pink vee-neck t-shirt and strappy sandals. Not exactly running clothes.

I know Jack is working a Saturday afternoon shift at the Blue Ridge Roast, and I'm hoping to surprise him. When I get into town and walk into the old industrial-style coffeehouse, he's nowhere to be seen. I walk up to the cash register and a handsome, mocha-skinned employee with a short, neat black beard greets me.

"What can I get you today?" he says, and his pearly white smile shines through the beard.

"I'm looking for Jack Crawley. Is he working today?"

Something changes in the way the barista is looking at me. His eyes study my face for an awkward amount of time before he finally says, "You're Avery, aren't you?"

"Yep, I am."

"I'm Andy Lincoln." He keeps his gaze squarely on me. It's almost like he knows something I don't know. "It's really a pleasure to meet you. Jack's taking out some trash. He should be back in the café soon."

I'm hardly listening to Andy. My mind is spinning wondering what he knows. Maybe Jack has a serious girlfriend. Maybe his serious girlfriend is the waitress pouring coffee a few tables over. The one with strawberry-blonde hair whose name tag reads "Daisy." Maybe Jack, Andy, and Daisy have a tight-knit work family and Andy is scared my presence in Black Mountain will threaten their little ecosystem. Maybe Andy hates change too.

I'm deep in my spiraling thoughts when I feel a tap on my shoulder. I'm so relieved to see Jack standing right there inches away, I don't even think. I leap into his arms and hug him like he is the only piece of glue holding what is left of me together.

"Hot damn, girl. You're even prettier than I remembered," Jack says with a full-dimple grin.

"Not so bad yourself." He looks cute in his little barista apron, and I hear the flirtatious edge to my voice.

I start to get nervous we'll be right back to the almost-kiss moment of New Year's Day and make a mental note to keep everything platonic. My parents are busy working on their relationship. They don't need Gran calling them to report I'm dating a townie.

"Andy, my man, I'm gonna take my break." Jack unties the apron and tosses it behind the counter. Then he holds out his arm and makes a little crook. "Shall we?"

We walk with our arms linked to our bench outside of the music school.

"So what sort of criminal activity do you have planned for us first?" I ask as we sit down. "We've never tried arson or grand theft auto."

"We've got all summer, Detective Walker," he says. "You're here for the whole thing, right?"

I pretend to tip a fake sheriff hat. "Yes, sir."

"So why don't we start with dinner." Now I am legit worried Jack might not be feeling platonic. But then he says, "Della is pestering me to have you over so she can cook for you. I told her how much you like banana pudding. She makes it with the little chess cookies on top."

I'm relieved. Dinner with his grandma's banana pudding is definitely a friend thing, not a romantic thing. "My mom is staying for the week, but next weekend, for sure, tell Della I'll be there."

"I thought your mom and Gran hated each other."

"Jack," I exclaim. "How did I forget to tell you about this?"

"Tell me what?"

"Oh, it's juicy, you're going to love it."

"Stop teasing, and spill." He punches my arm playfully.

"My parents' fighting all the time is no longer the most scandalous thing to hit the family." I get a devious little grin. I've probably delighted in the recent Margot drama a little bit too much, but it's nice not to be the cousin everybody pities for once.

I fill Jack in on the lurid details. "Margot was semi-arrested the night of her graduation."

"What the hell does semi-arrested mean?"

"It means she was in the car with some dudes who thought it would be funny to take a baseball bat and smash in the windows of a BMW parked at their rival school," I explain, reveling in the details of Margot's downfall.

"I don't get rich kids." Jack scratches his head.

"Turned out to be the vice principal's car, and turned out this vice principal is married to a lawyer." Jack laughs. "My Uncle Rey,

Margot's dad, is also a lawyer. Tons of drama later, five kids in the car and Margot's the only one without charges against her."

"Lucky Margot," Jack says.

"Well, I'm not sure she sees it that way." I finish up by saying, "She's supposed to go to the University of Miami next year, she has lots of family down there on her dad's side, and they are all super proud. Everybody's scared if she keeps hanging out with her crowd at home, she'll end up getting for-real arrested and lose her admission offer to Miami."

"So?"

"So she has to spend the whole summer with me at the cottage," I say with an unrestrained smirk.

"Because you're such a good influence?" Jack raises an eyebrow then grabs my phone out of my hand. "I'm going to call ol' Gran right now and tell her about the real Avery Walker. The trespassing badass."

I wrestle Jack to get my phone back, and by the time it is in my possession we are tangled on the bench, hands touching, but not quite holding each other.

There's a moment where I can hear both our breaths before Jack untangles and scoots away on the bench, but only a hair. It's the tiniest amount of space, but it's enough to move his body from the flirtatious zone to the friend zone. "Hey, so my break is over soon. Walk me back to work?"

"Sure." We make our way back to the Blue Ridge Roast. "If I'm going to get accepted to Boston University, then I need to study for my SAT subject test every day while I'm here this summer. Would it bother you if I brought my practice book to the coffee shop sometimes to study?"

"Are you serious? That would be great. Please do that every day. I'm working long hours this summer. I'd be so glad to get to see you." We reach the door. "I won't even be embarrassed my best friend is such a brainiac." He flashes me one of his cocky grins.

We say our good-byes, and he hugs me for the exact amount of time appropriate for a friend to hug another friend.

Because that is exactly what we are.

Two friends.

Two good friends.

CHAPTER TWENTY-FOUR

Sunday, May 29th

Mom, Gran, and I go to church in Black Mountain on Sunday morning. It's a beautiful morning, so we walk together down Oakley Road into downtown. When we pass Jack's house, he's sitting on his porch fiddling with his guitar. He gives me a little salute, and I return it with a subtle nod. My mom is still completely in the dark about my friendship with Jack. I don't know how to explain her "precious" daughter has been lurking around Black Mountain with a townie, trying to find the identity of her dead son's secret lover. It's much easier to keep the things I tell them ultra-light and undeniably happy. Like going to the prom with a Harvard-bound, future valedictorian.

When I sit down in the pew, my phone vibrates in my clutch. I glance down.

Violin-Jack: you look cute in yellow

Violin-Jack: Come to Blue Ridge Roast after church. I'll be working until close

Discreetly, I tap out a response while my gran and mom make small talk with the women in the pew behind us.

Me: Can't. Margot gets here this afternoon

Violin-Jack: Stay out of trouble, I don't want to have to use my tips as bail money.

122

Margot and Aunt Susan are sitting on the porch of the cottage when we arrive home from church. Everybody acts pleased to see each other, but nobody seems the slightest bit sincere.

I head downstairs to change out of my yellow church dress and Margot follows me with two suitcases. She throws them down on the bed in an aggressive heap and lets out a frustrated grunt.

"I'm sorry you have to spend your last summer before college here." I offer an olive branch. "I'm sure it's not what you wanted."

Margot gives me a not-so subtle look of annoyance. I hate the idea of spending an entire summer with someone who apparently can't stand the sight of me.

"What's your problem?" I ask.

Margot crosses her arms over her chest. "Excuse me?"

"You heard me. What's your problem?" I repeat.

She pinches her glossy lips and narrows her big chocolate eyes at me like I've lost my damn mind. She un-pinches her lips slightly like she is trying to figure out how to respond.

"We don't have to be like them." I gesture at the ceiling toward where my mom, Aunt Susan, and Gran are no doubt caught in a WASPy war of passive aggression. "Talk to me. Why do you hate me so much?"

She doesn't have to think to answer that. "I've never hated you."

"Okay, let me rephrase. Why have you always acted like you're so much better than me?"

"It's not what you think." She sits on her twin bed and looks at her feet.

"So talk. Do what our mothers can't ever seem to do. Say it like it is." I think about Jack and Della. They're so easy together. That's how a family should be.

"It feels really crass to say this since Whit is, you know..." Margot's voice trails off.

"Dead, Margot. Say he's dead." I finish her sentence for her.

"Whit is dead, and I wished for it to happen." Margot looks like she is going to cry.

"You wished for Whit to die?" This is not where I thought this conversation would go.

"Kind of." She bites her lip before she continues. "Last summer we were all here together. I was so jealous of you two. You had this easy friendship and I knew I'd never had it with anybody because I don't have a brother or a sister." She pauses and chooses her next words carefully. "One night last summer, Whit and I snuck out together and as we were walking back up the hill there was this huge full moon. It looked so close, I said I thought we could probably touch it."

These are the most words I have ever heard my cousin string together.

"Whit told me to make a wish on it and I wished you two didn't have each other because I was so jealous." She hangs her head down so I'm looking at the top of her shiny black hair. "It's my fault Whit died."

I laugh at this absurd admission.

"Margot, you're not that powerful." I sit next to her on the bed. "Whit took a traumatic blow to a tiny pinpoint in his frontal lobe. That's why he's dead. It has nothing to do with you. Or the moon."

"But it's how I've felt ever since I heard he died," Margot confesses. "It's why I feel too ashamed to really talk to you."

I look over at her, all tiny and contrite. For the first time, I see the lonely only child hiding under the tough popular-girl exterior. I hesitate for a moment but then swallow my pride and put my arm around her.

I squeeze her shoulder. "I had no idea you felt that way."

"I'm sorry you thought I hated you," she says.

"Look, I don't have Whit anymore. You're the closest thing I have to a sibling," I say. "Let's not be strangers this summer."

She nods and wipes a tear. "Do you really mean that?"

The perfect gesture to show Margot I mean what I am saying is to go over to my little dresser and pull Whit's phone out from under my socks. "Let me show you something."

I sit next to Margot and unlock the phone. I start at the beginning of the story and spill everything I know about OCMC. When I finish, Margot declares, "We should find this *chica* together."

"Um, about that." Now it is my turn to confess something. "So you know Jack Crawley, the guitar player who lives in town?"

"Oh yeah, total freak," Margot says with no hesitation. "You asked about him that night at the bonfire."

"Right, that's the one." I nod. "So, turns out he is kind of a freak, but he's my freak."

"*You* are dating Jack?" Her mouth hangs open in a perfect "O" after she asks this.

"No, no, no, god no," I clarify. "I'm not dating anybody. He's been helping me try to figure out who OCMC is, and what Whit wanted to tell me. We've become really good friends. We spent the whole winter break together last year, and we've stayed in touch."

"But you didn't find OCMC?" Margot clarifies.

"Nope, not even close. She's a ghost."

"Well, now I'm on the team." Margot sits up straight and fluffs her curls. "I don't lose. This will be my sole mission this summer. Time to make lemonade out of my lemons." Margot looks like she is on some imaginary campaign podium.

Jack is going to kill me.

CHAPTER TWENTY-FIVE

Monday, May 30ᵗʰ

After my morning run, Margot and I walk together to the Blue Ridge Roast. I have my SAT biology study guide in my tote and Margot is carrying a notebook with "OCMC" scrawled in her loopy handwriting across the cover.

When we get inside, I choose a green velvety chair in the front window with a big coffee table. Margot sits on the orange couch across from me. Jack spots us and hustles over with his cute little notepad to take our coffee orders.

I'm halfway through ordering my fancy frozen mocha when Jack interrupts me. "Why does your cousin have a notebook with those initials written on it?" he says it loud enough for me and Margot to hear him.

"I'm helping you two," Margot says in a chirpy voice. Jack raises his eyebrows at me. I wrinkle my nose and give him a puppy dog look. He shakes his head and then throws up his hands behind Margot's back. It reminds me of the silent conversations my parents used to have in the kitchen before their rough patch.

Jack heads back behind the counter, and within seconds my phone vibrates.

> *Violin-Jack: Since when are you and Margot pals? And since when does she know our secret?*
> *Me: It's not "our" secret. It's Whit's secret. Margot's not so bad. Give her a chance.*

I look up at Jack, who is squirting whipped cream in a little concentric circle. I watch him read my text from the counter. He mouths "Okay" from across the café, and I do a little pitter-patter motion over my heart so he knows I appreciate it.

***

The café stays busy through the morning, but by eleven Margot and I are the only patrons. Jack sits in the chair next to me, and Andy joins us. Before I can stop it, Margot is explaining everything about our little mission to Andy. In fairness, I'd hoped Jack would use Andy's private school connections to help us out, but more discreetly than how Margot is currently presenting things.

"So do you have any guesses, Andy?" Margot asks when she finishes giving him the full scoop.

"Nope. I'm not getting involved with that." Andy shakes his head. "Sounds kind of creepy to me, honestly."

"Well, you didn't know Whit," I state.

***

We follow the same pattern the next day. I wake up early for a run, then shower and change into something cute before walking to the Blue Ridge Roast, the OCMC notebook in Margot's arms, study guides in mine. We arrive at the perfect time for a post-morning rush to hang out with Andy and Jack.

When I first met Andy, I thought he was a little odd, but he's growing on me. As we chat, I notice how charming and artistic he is. He does all the chalkboards inside the café with extraordinary detail and design. The sandwich board sign outside has a drawing of a tall mountain and a little person on top sipping an iced coffee in a bathing suit surrounded by mountain snow. In detailed letters that put Margot's handwriting to shame it says "Beat the heat. Come on inside for iced coffee."

I learn Andy has been the day-shift manager at Blue Ridge Roast since he graduated high school three years ago. He lives on his own in a little apartment above a family's garage in downtown Black Mountain. His parents stopped supporting him when he declined admission to Wake Forest and decided to pursue a career in fine art. I like Andy and I notice Margot does too.

On Friday Andy asks for our coffee order and instead of answering her typical skinny iced vanilla latte, Margot asks, "Will you to be my date to the bonfire in Riverwalk Park tonight?"

Andy smiles warmly and perches himself on the edge of her chair. "Margot, you are beautiful, but I'm kind of hoping to take him out tonight." Andy winks then points to the newly hired waiter. "That's Spencer. He's covering while Daisy is out of town."

I admire Margot's confidence. I would never in a million years ask a boy out so boldly as she did, and then, when he rejects her, she sits up taller and even more confident. "Nice choice," she says. "I wish you two a lifetime of happiness or a weekend of hot make-out seshes, whichever you prefer. And I'll get my usual, skinny iced vanilla."

Andy nods and heads back to the counter to put the order in, but Jack is the one who brings us our drinks.

After the Friday morning rush, after the coffee house empties out, Andy and Jack join Margot and me at our seats in the front window. Margot barely lets them sit all the way down before she opens up her little notebook and starts talking. "So, folks, I've been jotting down lots of brilliant ideas all week for how we are going to find Whit's secret fling," she says with an air of self-importance. Jack's sitting on the arm of my green chair, so I'm not looking at his face, but I can feel his eyes rolling. I pinch the top of his thigh, warning him to be nice.

"Idea number one," Margot continues. "Do you have any jerseys with number eight or Walker on them, Avery? There's a bonfire party tonight, and if we go and you wear one, maybe she'll be there and spot you. Or anybody who knew him might make the connection and we could get more info."

Actually, it's not a terrible idea, but sadly I don't have any jerseys with me. I don't have time to tell Margot this before she goes into the next idea.

"Or, if we are feeling really bold, we could print his picture and carry it around asking people if they've seen this person to see if we get a reaction out of anyone."

"Like he's a kidnap victim?" Andy asks.

"Why do you care? You're not part of this," Margot snaps at Andy.

"I don't care. Besides, Spencer said yes to tonight." Andy grins.

"That's great. Are you going to bring him to the bonfire party?" I ask.

Andy quickly educates me. Bonfire parties are for high school kids. "I'm taking him to this little outdoor movie theater in Asheville. It's a big projector set up against a hillside, and you bring your own picnic. Spencer is really into outdoorsy stuff. I think he's going to like it."

"Shut up," Margot says and stands with her hand to her head like she's thinking really hard. "Shut up. Shut up."

We're all staring at Margot, trying to figure out what the heck is going on.

"Say that again," she finally says.

"But you told me to shut up."

"Say where you are taking Spencer tonight, please." Margot tries a softer tone.

"An outdoor movie theater called The Hill."

"Where it's all built into a hill, and bring your own food?" she asks.

"Yep," Andy confirms.

Margot takes a deep breath and looks around to be sure all eyes are on her before she speaks. "Y'all, Whit went to that outdoor movie theater a few summers ago. He told me about it when we snuck out together. He was carrying a bag of leftovers and I kept pestering him about why he snuck out with leftovers. Then I was so impressed perfect jock Whit was going somewhere hip. Maybe he went there with OCMC?"

We all let the information sink in and then Margot announces she thinks we should tag along on Andy and Spencer's date to look for clues.

"Uh, no," Andy says firmly.

"I'm with Andy on this one," I say. "It's a nice thought, but I can't imagine there would be any helpful information. It's been years, it's not like she's sitting there waiting for Whit."

"You're wrong," Jack says after being quiet through the whole conversation. "That's exactly what you said about hiking Graybeard, and then Whit sent us a sign while we were there. I think we should go to The Hill tonight and see what happens."

"Great, it's settled then." Margot smiles smugly like she's won something. A customer walks in, and both Andy and Jack get back to work. I turn my attention back to the SAT study book for a few minutes until I see Jack standing alone at the cash register. I get up to talk to him.

"Since when do you side with Margot?" I ask.

"Since she had a good idea," he answers.

"You honestly think that's a good idea? Like you really believe we'll find something?"

"Of course not." He leans across the counter so he can whisper. "But I miss you and I want to go do something adventurous with you."

"I've seen you every day since I've been in Black Mountain, how can you miss me?"

"It's not the same when I'm at work, and you're with Margot. Plus Andy is right. The bonfire parties are for townie kids. If I'm going to hang out with you, I'd rather go somewhere classier."

I raise my eyebrows. "So we're classy now?"

"Meet at my house, and I'll borrow Della's truck."

I fidget with my ponytail then give in. It sounds more fun than going to the bonfire and watching the girls from last Christmas throw themselves at Jack.

"It's a date, Walker," Jack says before getting back to work.

CHAPTER TWENTY-SIX

Friday, June 3rd

When we arrive at The Hill, Spencer and Andy are seated on a big quilt spread over a little spot on the hillside. We start to spread out our own blanket in a spot on the other side of the hill, but Spencer says it's silly and insists we all sit together. As we all scoot together Andy shoots us dirty looks while Spencer isn't watching. "Sorry," I mouth across the blanket.

But it turns out Spencer is way more fun when he isn't bussing breakfast plates and coffee mugs. He and I bond over both being from Tennessee. He's from right outside of Knoxville and just graduated high school. He explains he's working and staying in Black Mountain this summer with some relatives so he can do some hiking.

"I've actually done all nine hundred miles of trails of the Smoky Mountains," he says like it's no big deal. "I decided to spend some time out here before college and do some of the Blue Ridge hikes." Andy looks totally smitten.

He's the only one of us who's over twenty-one. He offers to buy a pitcher of beer from the little concession stand. Margot and Spencer looked pleased, but Jack says, "No cup for me, dude," as Andy leaves the group.

I lean and whisper, "Really? I would've bet my life you're a beer drinker."

"You would've been wrong," he whispers back.

I've never tasted beer, but I let Andy pour me a little plastic cup even though I plan to slide it over to Margot the moment she finishes her first. We're quiet for the movie, but as soon as it's over, our group becomes so loud and goofy, the two sober people, Jack and me, can't quite follow what's so funny.

We turn our backs to everyone, and we're looking out over the hills.

"Did you turn down beer so I wouldn't be the only sober person?" I ask.

"Nope," Jack says.

"Because you're driving?"

"Sure." It's not like him to give one-word answers.

"Are you going to elaborate?" I prod.

"Both my parents are addicts. That shit is genetic." He stares at the hills. "Plus, Della would kill and bury me at Graceland if I ever came home smelling like booze. Cigarettes are fine. Girls are fine. But she's already been through the pain of addiction with my dad. She'd rather kill me than go through that again."

"I'm sorry. I didn't know any of that." I put my hand on his.

"That's because I've never told anybody before." He stops staring at nothing and looks right at me. I feel a warm affection swelling inside my heart. Of all the people in the world, he trusted me with this information. I look back at him, and we hold each other's stare.

I know he's never going to make a move, not after last Christmas when I shot him down at Della's truck. But with this warmth beating inside my chest, I don't know if I'll be able to resist leaning in for a kiss. I don't have time to fully process my feelings when my drunken cousin flings her arms around Jack and me, and demands he takes us home.

"Avery, it's eleven-oh-six, we have to be home by eleven-thirty or we are never going to be allowed out of the house again." I'm more concerned about the way Margot smells than curfew, but she's right, we need to get home.

"Let's go, ladies," Jack says as we start to head out. "Behave yourselves, gentlemen," he shouts over his shoulder to Spencer and Andy.

We pile in the truck, and smelly Margot sits between Jack and me. After the moment on the hill has passed, I'm thankful she interrupted. If she hadn't, I might've done something to jeopardize my friendship with Jack.

He's the steadiest person in my life, and I can't risk losing that.

I   hate   change.

CHAPTER TWENTY-SEVEN

Saturday, June 4ᵗʰ

Mom and Aunt Susan leave for their respective homes first thing in the morning. But not before giving us a quick lecture. There's no way they didn't smell the beer on Margot's breath last night, but in this family, we avoid conflict at all costs. Instead of calling Margot out for her boozy evening, they talk to us about obeying curfew, making good choices, and respecting Gran. Aunt Susan ends the lecture with a stern, "Especially you, Margot."

As soon as her mother's back is turned, Margot leans in close and whispers, "If they only knew which cousin is the one who spent practically every night of winter break at a boy's house." My eyes bug out, and I give her a pleading look to not betray me. She doesn't.

Margot is definitely growing on me.

Mom's car is barely out of the driveway when my phone buzzes with a text from Jack.

Violin-Jack: Della wants to know if you can come over for dinner tonight at 7.

Me: Sure, sounds good.

I see the little bubbles to indicate he's writing. They stop. Go again. Stop. Go again. I know Jack well enough to know he's thinking hard about what he wants to say. I wonder if he spent the whole night thinking about that moment between us like I did.

Does this dinner invite mean something?

A new text finally comes through, but it's not what I expected.

Violin-Jack: Della invited Andy so if Margot wants to come, that's cool. Plenty of food and stuff.

My turn to type. Stop. Type. Stop. I guess the dinner invite means a sweet grandmother who cooks well and wants to feed her grandson's friends, nothing more. After typing a hundred different responses, I finally land on:

Cool, I'll bring her. See you at 7.

***

As Margot and I walk to 88 Oakley Road, I'm trying to decide if I should prepare Margot for the Elvis shrine or let her be surprised. "Have I ever told you about Jack's grandma, Della?"

"No, not really," Margot says. "Only that he lives with her because his parents abandoned him or something." The way Margot says this, and the tone of voice she uses, feels snobby and judgmental. A surge of protection toward Della and Jack swamps me.

"There's a lot more to the story," I say quickly even though the truth is I don't know the story. Not really. I know Jack's parents brought him to Dollywood when they were happy, and that he rarely talks about them. After last night, I know about their addiction. Which makes me think about our "moment." Feeling awkward, I change the subject.

"Do you know who Elvis is?"

"What type of question is that?" Margot scoffs. "Are there people who don't know who Elvis is?"

"Sorry, dumb question. Della is like really into Elvis. It's a whole thing. Her brother met him in Germany, and then he passed away, her brother, not Elvis, although I guess Elvis did die too." I am rambling nervously. "Point of the story is, they both died and now Della is really into Elvis." Margot is staring at me like I've lost my mind.

"Why are you so nervous?" she calls me out.

I really don't know. Perhaps I'm worried Margot will be a snob and judge Jack and Della when she sees their home. Maybe I'm worried Jack and my "moment" last night meant something. Or maybe I'm worried the moment meant nothing. I almost tell Margot everything, but we reach the stone steps to Jack's house before I can think of the right words.

As we arrive, Andy is climbing out of his little banged-up Saturn. We climb the steps together and Andy says, "You ever met Della before, Margot?"

"Why does everybody keep asking me that?" She humpfs, then she reaches the porch and I watch her eyes pop open, taking it all in. "Wow," she mouths silently. To my relief, she's admiring, not judging. I take a deep breath, and when Jack joins us, his presence makes me feel calm. Even after last night, his big, confident energy, and his little crooked dimples put me at ease. He makes me feel more like myself than I feel when I'm alone.

We all help Jack set the big table on the porch with Elvis plates, Elvis cloth napkins, and utensils with tiny little Kings lining them. Della brings out a delicious Southern meal: ham, potato salad, and corn on the cob. She makes me promise to save room for banana pudding. I ask her to tell Margot the story about Elvis and her brother, and it's even better the second time around.

"Hey, Della," I say when she finishes. "I need to confess something."

"What could you possibly need to confess? Does it have anything to do with sneaking in my window every night last Christmas?" She winks and smiles at me.

"No, ma'am." My cheeks flush with pink. "When you told me that story, it meant a lot to me, and I should've told you why, but I wasn't ready to talk about my brother yet."

She takes my hand gently. "Jack told me about Whit, dear. I'm so sorry, and I'm glad my story meant something to you. Do you have an Elvis?"

"Pardon?"

"Do you have something that makes Whit feel alive to you? What did you call it, dear, the reminiscence bump?" Della asks, recalling the term I taught her and Jack at Christmas.

"Yes," I say. "Actually, Jack has been helping me try to solve a little mystery about Whit. He's helped me keep him alive." My hands are folded in my lap, and Jack reaches under the table and puts his hand over mine and squeezes tight.

"That makes this old grandma's heart happy to hear." Della gets up from the table and starts to clear dishes. "You four stay put and enjoy each other. I'll excuse myself so you can talk without having to censor yourselves for my old lady ears."

"Thank you, Della, the food was delicious," Andy, Margot, and I all shout over each other. We all help clear the table then make our way back out to the porch.

We sit and listen as Andy fills us in on his date with Spencer. It is clear that the two really hit it off. "Have you called or texted him yet?" Margot asks. When Andy says no, Margot demands he get out his phone, and they put their heads together to craft the perfect post-first-date text.

While they are busy, I turn to Jack. "Hey."

"Hey."

"So, you told Della about me sneaking in?" I ask playfully.

"Swear I didn't." He puts up his hands in a gesture of innocence. "She's smarter than us, I guess. I bet the Elvis wind chime gave you away."

"About that," I say.

"About the Elvis wind chime?"

"No, Jack. About me sleeping over here."

"Yeah?"

"Well, I'm doing better with my grief. I've actually slept fine at the cottage so far this week, and because of Margot, Gran's keeping an eye on us. I don't think I'm going to be able to sneak out much over the summer," I explain. The truth is, I keep thinking about that moment at the movies, alone in the dark with him, and I don't trust myself to not risk our friendship.

Our brief moment of privacy ends before Jack has a chance to say anything.

"Guess what?" Margot interrupts. "I made Andy invite Spencer over here, and wait for it... he's coming. In like ten minutes."

Andy's trying to act annoyed, but he can't fake it. A big smile is spreading across his face. "Do you mind, Jack, if Spencer joins us?"

"Of course not, dude. Way to go." Jack high-fives Andy, then turns to me and picks up our conversation, only now we have an audience. "I actually don't think it's a good idea for you to sneak over here. I'm relieved you're not going to try."

I'm surprised, I fully expected Jack to list every reason in the book why I better start sneaking in his window every night again.

"I do not get these two," Andy whispers to Margot.

"Nobody does," Margot whispers back.

"I kind of thought you would try to talk me into it like you did over Christmas." I slump my shoulders and then lie. "But no worries, I'm glad we're on the same page."

"Y'all have a seriously strange arrangement." Andy points one finger at me and one at Jack. It makes me think about the day I met Andy, and how it seemed he knew something I didn't.

"I think our situation is pretty clear," I say defensively. "We're friends."

"Right," Jack says. "Also, pen pals, don't forget pen pals." Jack gives Andy a look as he says "pen pals," but I can't quite read what it's supposed to mean.

"Okay, folks, time to behave yourselves," Andy says in a hushed voice directed at me and Jack. Then he stands up and shouts, "Up here, Spencer."

Spencer joins us, and Andy greets him with a sweet side hug and a peck on the cheek. Spencer is delightful as ever, and before long he convinces Jack to get out his violin. It's been four years since I've heard Jack play, but it takes me back to that skinny nerd hiding underneath the overconfident charmer. He plays "If You're Gonna Play in Texas (You've Got to Have a Fiddle in the Band)," and we're all singing at the top of our lungs, laughing so loud we can hear it echoing down the mountain.

Suddenly it's eleven p.m. and Margot and I are hugging everybody good-bye so we can make it back to the cottage before curfew. When I hug Jack, he pulls me close and kisses the top of my head then he says into my hair, "I wouldn't kick you out if you snuck over, you know. I just don't want to be the guy who gets you in trouble."

"I know," I say so quietly into his chest, I'm not sure he hears me. Then Margot pulls my hand to head down the steps, and we sprint home.

As we run off, I hear Andy shout, "Y'all better come back and do this again."

With his declaration, a tradition is born.

CHAPTER TWENTY-EIGHT

Saturday, June 11ᵗʰ

Nearly every night last week, our little group ate delicious food on Della's porch. It always ended with us cajoling Jack to get out his violin or guitar, and everybody sang and danced like fools. We filled in Spencer about our mission to find OCMC, and much to Andy's dismay, Spencer completely disagreed our mission is creepy. He declared it "the most tragically romantic story ever." We all took turns throwing out outlandish theories about who it could be in hopes something would stick.

"Maybe OC stands for Orange County," Margot suggested.

"Orange County Math Club," I tossed out. "Whit was humiliated to be in love with a math nerd, so he kept her a secret."

"Orange County Methodist Church," Spencer added, eliciting a flirtatious eye roll from Andy.

"Orange County Musical Choir," Jack said, and we all shook our heads, so Jack continued, "Maybe it was a secret because OCMC is married and old."

"Maybe she's a MILF?" Margot clasped her hands together. "One Cute MILF Catch." Andy shook his head with disapproval every time the conversation headed this direction. But I loved it. I loved not being alone in keeping Whit's unfinished business alive. It made it feel like he's still real, and he still matters.

Sometimes, when the evening reached the pinnacle of joyfulness, I floated out of my body and looked down at the scene. It's like I could hover there and see myself belting out lyrics, holding Jack's hand, confiding in Margot, all these experiences I never knew I was missing.

Dead Sibling Society #9: When I have transformative moments, I feel guilty my dead sibling won't have his own transformative experiences.

The summer is the perfect recipe for big life moments. Take a seventeen-year-old girl, a beautiful mountain setting, two parents fighting, and sprinkle in a new group of friends. Yep. I end up with all these little moments of evolution.

It's like when you poke holes in a blackout curtain. At first, there are tiny little rays of sunlight in the mostly dark space, but if you keep poking, your whole room becomes bright and shiny.

I wonder if Whit ever had a chance at these moments before he died. In my mind, I can picture him and a shadowy outline of OCMC sitting at Graybeard's overlook.

Did Whit know what it's like to be seventeen and float above your own body?

I hope so.

***

Tonight, Margot and I are saying our good-byes to the rest of the group so we can make it home by curfew when Spencer stops us. "Hey wait," he says as we start to head down the stone steps. "Before you go, what are you guys doing on Monday? I looked at the schedule and me, Jack, and Andy all have Monday off."

"Oh, I don't know. Let me look at me and Avery's super-busy calendar of bumming around the café and playing cards with our grandmother," Margot says sarcastically as she sits down. "What do you know? We're free. What do you have in mind?"

"Do you guys like amusement parks?" Spencer asks.

We all nod eagerly to hear what he has planned.

"Pretty much everybody in Knoxville has some sort of Dollywood connection, and I have six free tickets that expire at the end of June. This is my last weekend off before they expire. I'm thinking mini road trip." He seems bashful as if he is worried we might say no.

But Margot and Andy immediately start chanting, "Dollywood. Dollywood. Dollywood." But Jack's shaking his head. I'm the only person who knows why.

"Sorry, y'all, Jack hates Dollywood," I say nonchalantly, trying to make it sound like it's no big deal.

"I don't hate Dollywood," Jack says and kicks me in the shin under the table. "I avoid it because it brings up my parents and crappy stuff." I'm surprised he is mentioning his parents. Damn it. I've mostly managed to keep how I feel about Jack in the friend zone the past couple of weeks. But watching him be vulnerable strips me down, and the warm affection rises up from where I've kept it buried.

Andy says, "Well, Jack my boy," I can tell he is tipsy from the joy of his budding romance, "Dolly Parton is a national treasure and I will not stand for you not knowing the joy of her hillbilly amusement park. We are going to reclaim Dollywood for you."

Margot, Andy, and Spencer begin chanting, "Reclaim Dolly. Reclaim Dolly. Reclaim Dolly."

I look at Jack, who isn't amused. I can't imagine doing a road trip without him. "Please," I mouth, and then add, "For me." He narrows his eyes, but then slowly the little dimples start to pop out and he smiles.

"What the hell." He stands up. "I'm reclaiming Dolly."

Everybody else stands up to cheer and jump around like our team won the Super Bowl. But I stay in my seat. I can't quite move. Holy crap. I have power over Jack, and it scares me.

When things calm down, Spencer reminds us that there are five of us and he has a sixth ticket. "Anybody else we should bring?" he asks.

"Oh my god," Margot says. "That's only like three hours from Nashville, you should totally get Riley to meet us there." She turns to the group. "Riley is Avery's best friend, but she is so much cooler than Avery. No offense." Whenever Margot has spent time at our home in Nashville, she and Riley have always gotten a kick out of each other. It used to drive me nuts, but now I see what Riley saw in Margot: she keeps things interesting.

I roll my eyes at Margot's jab, though she isn't wrong. I really miss my best friend and would love it if she could come.

"It'd make reclaiming Dollywood a whole lot more fun if I get to finally meet the infamous Riley," Jack says and rubs his hands together. "Come on, Avery. You outed my Dollywood problem. You owe me."

"All right, all right. I'll text her and let you know." I hold up my phone so Margot can see the time.

"Bye, bee-atches. We've got to go." Margot gives everybody air kisses. "See y'all Monday for the world's most epic mini-vacay to Dollywood."

CHAPTER TWENTY-NINE

Monday, June 13th

Our alarm clock rings at 6:30 a.m. It's a two-hour drive to Dollywood, and Spencer assures us we'll have way more fun if we are there first thing when the park opens before it gets crowded. Margot and I laid out clothes the night before. I convinced her that "athleisure" and sneakers are the way to go for a full day at Dollywood. No way would I wear a dress and wedges. The five of us meet at Blue Ridge Roast at 7 a.m., grab a quick coffee on the house, and pile into Andy's Saturn.

Spencer sits in the front with Andy, which leaves me, Margot, and Jack in the back. They announce since I have skinny little runner hips, I'm the one who should sit in the middle seat. Jack stretches out and puts his arm around me before laying his big head on my shoulder.

"Power nap time, Walker." He closes his eyes and his thick black hair tickles my neck the whole drive. While Jack sleeps, everybody else sings along to Dolly tunes, since, as Andy declared, she's a national treasure.

When we arrive, Riley's Jeep is already parked near the front of the big amusement park lot. It's been less than a month since I left Nashville, but I feel a strong need to hug my best friend. I climb across Jack's lap and pop open the door before Andy barely puts the car in park. Riley and I squeal and hug, and squeal some more. When Jack finally post-nap stumbles out of the car, he stretches and lumbers over to Riley. Without any hesitation, he wraps his big body around her tiny frame and hugs her tight. When he lets go, we do proper introductions and start to walk to the park.

Riley loops her arm through mine and holds me back from the group for a minute.

"Avery Walker. Dang, girl," she whisper-screams. "Jack is so effing hot. Like I mean I've seen him in pictures, but damn. I wasn't prepared for that much man."

I shrug like I'm not sure if he's that hot, when, of course, I know he absolutely is.

"If the cheer squad at WPA knew *that* is who you're spending your summer with, you'd have a dozen new best friends all begging to do sleepovers at your gran's cottage."

"You need to calm down," I say. Jack looks over his shoulder and sees we're lagging, and he pauses to wait. When we catch up to him, he gets between us and puts one arm around Riley, and one arm around me. That sneaky warm feeling keeps building in my heart. Now he's being sweet to my best friend.

"Take a picture for me to send to Will," Riley shouts at Jack and tosses him her phone. We do a silly pose in front of Dolly Parton's signature butterfly, and Riley whispers in my ear, "I already love Jack."

***

The day is a whirlwind of more belly laughs than I've had since I joined the "Dead Sibling Society." As we get off the Wild Eagle roller coaster, I look over at Jack and see his expression is filled with pure adrenaline and joy. I stand on my tiptoes to whisper in his ear, "You reclaimed Dolly, didn't you?" Instead of saying yes, he lifts me off the ground, flops me over his shoulder, and twirls me around.

When my feet hit the ground, I grab his hand and make him look me in the eye. "Seriously, Crawley. How are you feeling?"

"I'm busy making more happy memories to haunt me forever." His grin is genuine, and I'm glad. I spot Riley watching us. She smiles and shakes her head. Her look says, "I cannot believe quiet Avery Walker is flirting with the hottest guy at Dollywood."

One of my favorite parts of the day is watching as Riley and Jack click. I've always known they'd like each other, but watching it play out is such a treat.

All six of us fit in one raft for the Wild River Rampage. As we spin our circle around, dodging and hitting various water spouts and splashing rapids, Jack keeps leaning over top of me like he is protecting me from the splashes, but then pulls away at the last minute, leaving me the wettest person in the raft. Every time, he laughs at his own antics, and by the time we climb out of the ride, I'm soaked to the bone. Jack is barely damp.

"I'm sorry, poor little Avery." He pulls his dry shirt over the top of his head, and then pats me dry with it. Riley mouths "whoa" when she sees Jack's abs.

"Give me that shirt, Crawley." I take it out of his hand. "I'm going to strangle you right here." I chase him playfully, swatting the shirt at him.

"Okay, you two," Spencer says. "I'm so confused. Are y'all like a couple or what's the deal?"

I stop swatting at Jack and hand him his shirt back. "We're friends." Andy and Margot make a "guffaw" noise.

"So you're not dating anybody?" Spencer directs his question at me. I shake my head.

"Does that mean I could set you up with someone?" Spencer asks excitedly. "I have a straight younger brother, and he's coming to visit Black Mountain next week."

"Oh, Grayson would be perfect for Avery," Andy jumps into the conversation.

"Do you even know this guy?" Jack asks Andy.

"No, but I've heard enough about him," Andy says as he puts his arm around Spencer to prove their couple-hood.

"Good luck with that," Riley says. "I've literally been pushing boys on Avery since we were thirteen. She's never interested."

"I think I might be interested in a straight version of Spencer," I say, even though after today it's near impossible to convince myself Jack is only a friend. "Tell me about him."

Spencer and Andy both clap and tell me he's smart like me and wants to go far away to college like me, and Spencer is totally going to give him my number.

We make our way to a table in the park where we eat a late dinner before the fireworks start. We gorge on hot dogs, nachos, and cotton candy, because…why not? The sun slowly disappears over the Smoky Mountains, and Spencer says he knows the best spot in the park to sit and watch Dolly's fireworks.

Everybody gets up and throws away our piles of junk food wrappers. We follow Spencer, who's holding Andy's hand. Margot and Riley walk arm in arm behind them, and the glow of the sunset makes the whole scene look like it's straight out of a movie. As I watch my friends walk down the amusement park path, I realize how much I've missed the feeling of a family over the past few months.

Today feels so good, and I hope it's been the same for Jack.

I turn around because I want to check how he's doing, and he's still sitting at the picnic table. "Hey, Crawley, aren't you coming?"

He doesn't say anything, but stands up and starts to follow me toward the rest of our group. We take a few steps before his strong hand reaches out from behind me and gently grabs my shoulder. "Wait a second."

I stop and turn to face him.

"Please don't go out with Spencer's idiot brother." He puts both arms on my shoulder and gently tilts up my chin and looks me in the eye. "If you're ready to date somebody. Please, date me."

Gulp.

"I know all the reasons you want to be friends. I know it's been less than a year since Whit died, and things aren't easy in your life right now, but I can't stop how I feel about you. You're not only my best friend. You're everything." There's a long moment of silence then Jack whispers softly in my ear. "Please say something. Anything. You're killing me here."

This is the moment where I can't be a Walker. I can't sweep how I feel about Jack under a rug for another minute. But I also can't think of a single word to encompass how deeply I feel about him.

My mind races, and I come up blank. So, instead of saying anything, I stand on the very tips of my toes, wrap my hands around Jack's neck, pull his face closer to mine, and kiss him. The kiss is warm and deep, nothing like the first time I kissed him four years ago. To my surprise and delight, he kisses me back with as much passion.

We stand there, in the middle of the crowded Dollywood path, locked in a steamy kiss, six months in the making.

He pulls his lips away from mine long enough to ask, "Is this really happening?"

"I don't want to talk." I take his hand and lead him out of the middle of the path to an empty bench. We have a long history with benches.

We sit as close as two people can sit and continue kissing. We might not be with the rest of the group, but this bench is the best spot in the whole world to watch the booming fireworks while making a few fireworks of our own.

"What made you change your mind?" Jack whispers in my ear, his lips grazing my neck.

I pull his lips toward mine and punctuate each word with a deep kiss. "Della." Kiss. "Riley." Kiss. "OCMC." Kiss.

"You're listing other women," Jack says between lip-locks.

"It's the way you treat people," I say before taking a break from the dreamy make-out session. "There is nothing sexier than somebody who loves his grandma, is kind to my best friend, and cares about my dead brother's secret lover."

"Well, that last one is on every girl's list." Jack laughs.

"It's true though, you know." I hold his face in my hands, my thumbs resting beside each dimple. "You made it impossible to be friends." He puts one hand behind my head, and we stare at each other's features like we've never really seen each other until this moment.

"I don't want to ever leave this bench, but if we want a ride home, we probably need to find everybody else." Jack runs his hands through my hair as he speaks. "Your hair smells like the beach, you know."

"Really, the beach. Is that good?"

"It's the best smell in the world. Like coconuts and sunshine," he says. "I've always wanted to tell you that, but I thought it would sound too creepy."

He leans in closer and exaggerates inhaling deeply. We both start laughing, and when we make eye contact, we laugh even more. Eventually, we peel ourselves from our bench and walk hand in hand to find the group.

"So what happens next?" I ask as we scan the crowd.

"Next? I take you out to dinner tomorrow tonight when I get off work."

"A date?"

"Yes, a real first date. I pick you up, I meet your gran, the whole thing."

Kissing and holding hands at Dollywood feels like an entirely different thing than Jack Crawley knocking on the door of Huckleberry Cottage.

Dollywood is like a fantasy world and Huckleberry Cottage is where my real live judgmental Gran will be waiting to examine everything about Jack and report back to the rest of the family.

"Maybe," I answer.

There's no time for Jack to react to my lukewarm answer. Our friends jump up behind us, chattering and shouting over each other, and reliving the "best night ever." Nobody notices Jack's arm wrapped tight around my waist, and of course, they wouldn't because that's how Jack and I have always been. But this time it's different. It's like he and I are the only ones who know this for one small slice of a moment.

Slowly, we make our way back to the parking lot, and I give Riley a big hug. She's spending the night with a friend from Warner Prep who goes to UT Knoxville. The rest of us are headed back to Black Mountain. Gran extended curfew to account for the two-hour drive.

As I hug Riley close, I whisper in her ear, "Jack and I kissed."

"It's about damn time," she whispers back, then slaps my butt in a cheeky way.

"Be safe tonight, promise?"

"No, you be safe, Avery." She lets go of me and turns her attention to Jack. "Hurt this girl, and I will hunt you down and beat you with your damn violin. Got it?"

"Got it, chief." Jack gives Riley a hug then we all pile into the Saturn.

Everybody but Andy is quiet. While he blasts "Jolene" over and over to keep himself awake, I replay the whole day in my head like a highlight reel. I replay Jack asking me on a date for tomorrow, and think hard about it. Then I tug on his shoulder until he opens his eyes. "Hey, you. I'll go on that date with you tomorrow."

"You don't care if your family knows you're dating the townie freak?" he mumbles as he slowly wakes up.

"Nope. I want them all to know." I kiss his shoulder.

"Really?" His eyes are fully open and alert.

"Yes, really."

He raises his voice to be heard over top of Dolly's vocals. "Hey, Margot, I'm dating your cousin." Margot sleepily reaches her arm across me and hits him, so he shouts louder. "Me, the townie freak you warned Avery about. I'm dating her now, and she doesn't care if you know."

He looks at me, watching for my reaction to see if I actually meant what I said.

I shrug like it's all no big deal. Margot wakes up enough to say, "Hate to disappoint you, but the fact you two are hookin' up surprises absolutely no one."

Jack leans over and kisses me deeply. "Gross," Margot shouts and swats us both. Andy and Spencer are laughing and holding hands in the front seat. "At this point, you're all rubbing it in my face that I'm the only sad single person in the car."

We all say some version of, "Oh poor, beautiful, Margot" and then we're back to quiet. I bury my head in Jack's chest, and he kisses the top of it and mumbles, "Coconuts and sunshine."

It all feels so right. Any fear I had about the change in our friendship, the change in what my family might think, the change of being a girl who's actually dating Jack—is gone.

I leave it behind at the Tennessee-North Carolina border and squeeze his hand tighter.

This right here—this is a good change.

CHAPTER THIRTY

Tuesday, June 14ᵗʰ

"How was Dollyland?" Gran asks over lunch since Margot and I slept through breakfast.

I try to act like a normal tired and surly teenager, but I can't stop smiling. "So good," I answer in a singsong voice.

"What's on the agenda for today now that you've slept half of it away?" Gran asks as she tersely cuts her hard-boiled egg with a knife.

"Avery has a date," Margot answers. Gran sets down her knife and flattens her lips into a straight line. I shoot eyeball daggers at Margot. I didn't have a plan yet for broaching the subject, and this wouldn't have been it.

"And are you allowed to date, Avery Jane?"

"Gran, I'm seventeen." I take a sip of my Diet Coke, praying she doesn't interpret that as backtalk.

"Right, I forget sometimes." She sighs. "So, did Margot introduce you to a local boy?"

"Sort of." I choose my words carefully. I meant everything I said in the car last night, I don't give a damn what my uppity family thinks of him, but I also don't want Gran to lock me up in the cottage, or worse, send me back to Nashville to protect me from what she'll think is the local hoodlum. "His name is Jack Crawley. He's a musician. We've been friends for a few years. I like to walk in the park downtown, and that's where he gives music lessons. In that old blue Victorian house."

Nothing I've said is untrue, and I hope it paints a picture of a band kid in Gran's head instead of a vandal. "He's going to pick me up at seven tonight, and we're going to go into town for some pizza. It's really no big deal."

"All right. Remember to be home by eleven-thirty."

Whew. That went so much better than I thought it would.

After lunch, I go for a run and get completely lost in my thoughts. Like why do we spend so much time fearing the judgmental glare of Gran? Instead of thinking of Jack, the whole thing makes me think of OCMC.

I wonder if Whit was scared of what Gran and the family would think. I wish I could shout back in time and say he should tell us all about her. Maybe that one tiny change would've been enough to fix everything.

What if OCMC hadn't been a secret? Maybe Whit would've called her before the game on the third Friday of October. He would've had her on his mind, and played a few seconds slower than he did.

Even if he still got hit, maybe the hit would've been delayed enough to have touched another point in his brain.

No more secrets, no more sweeping all the uncomfortable truths under the rug, Avery.

I make a silent little vow to myself. If I'm going to really date Jack, I can't carry on the Walker family tradition of hiding everything.

***

Margot helps me put together my outfit: a caramel-colored tank top with skinny jeans and an oversize black cardigan. She takes my hair out of my signature low ponytail and gives me loose beach curls with her curling wand before applying a full face of makeup to my pale complexion. "That townie isn't going to know what hit him," Margot says, patting herself on the back.

When Jack arrives exactly at seven, it's the first time he's pulled Della's truck down the gravel driveway all the way up to the cottage. Anytime he's picked me up or dropped me off before, he's parked down the road.

He's effortlessly charming with Gran, but I can't help but notice she doesn't take her eyes off Della's beat-up blue truck. Gran buys a shiny new Cadillac every two years, and has for my entire life.

The moment Jack and I are alone on the porch, ready to head into town, he stops and snaps a picture of me with his old flip phone. "What are you doing?" I ask. "I didn't even know that thing could take pictures."

"Barely, it's grainy, but it'll still help me remember how you look tonight," he says then helps me into the truck. We head to Black Mountain Mill and Pizzeria, and when we walk in the front door, the hostess shouts "Crawley" over-enunciating the "lee" syllable with the same vocal fry popular girls like Caroline Daniel use. She leaps out from behind her hostess stand and wraps her arms around Jack's neck. "Where have you been all summer?"

"Working a lot, mostly," Jack answers.

"At the Blue Ridge Roast, right? Maybe I should stop by and see you sometime." She twirls her fake blonde hair around her finger and seems to forget her hostess duties entirely.

"Table for two, please," Jack says, ignoring the come-on. It's only then that the hostess notices me. She tones the flirting down a bit, but I must not look too threatening because she still bats her eyelashes as she seats us and fusses over how good it is to see "Crawley."

"That hostess is awfully…flirty," I say as we sit down. "Any chance she seduces out-of-town football players and has secret love affairs with them?"

Jack scratches his chin. "Her name is Bella Bunch. Two B's, no O, M, or C. Plus, I know for sure it's not her."

"Uh, excuse me, sir," I say. "How do you know for sure?"

"Come on, I don't want to talk about Bella." Jack shakes his head at me and then changes the subject. "I'm really excited to see what Avery Walker is like on a date."

"So am I." I laugh. "You know this is basically like my first date, right?"

"Really?" He puts down the plastic menu and reaches across the table to hold my hand.

"The last time I went on a date was the Friday night that Whit got hurt," I say, looking at my menu instead of meeting Jack's gaze.

"You've never told me that story," Jack says. I realize this is the point in the date where he expects me to tell him.

"There's not much to say really. I went to the football game with this guy named Henry. Before I could get over my nerves and even talk to him, I was leaving the game to chase an ambulance to the emergency room." I take a sip of water. "Henry never texted or called, or talked to me at school the whole semester. So my bar for dates is set pretty low."

"Wait. This shady dude didn't even text you to see if you were okay?" Jack looks genuinely upset on my behalf.

"Nope." I shake my head. "Never a word."

"If I lived in Nashville, I'd kick this idiot's ass." Jack hits his fist in his other hand. Total cheese.

"Last night Riley said that if you lived in Nashville you'd be dating all the Warner Prep cheerleaders, not me." I change the subject from the whole embarrassing Henry story.

"Riley did not say that," Jack challenges.

"Well, not in those exact words, but she's not wrong. If we went to the same school, there is no way you'd ever even notice me." I twist a curl around my finger like the hostess did. "This isn't exactly how I dress at school."

"First of all, we both know I'd get kicked out of a fancy school like yours. But, more importantly, I think it would be the other way around," Jack says.

"What do you mean?"

"I think you'd be way too good for me if we went to the same school. You probably wouldn't even know I existed." Jack takes a sip of his water and then keeps going. "I attend the bare minimum to keep truancy officers out of Della's hair. I've never taken an honors class in my life. I doubt anybody even expects me to graduate next year."

I've never really thought about any of this, and I'm not sure how to respond. We both turn to the menu and change the topic to pizza. We order a "Carnivore," and while we're waiting my phone vibrates in my clutch.

Because I always assume the worst when my phone rings, I answer it. "Everything okay?" I ask, skipping hello.

"Yep, just checking in on your date."

"I'm on it, and hanging up on you." I click the phone off then turn my attention back to Jack.

"It was Riley." I rub my temples, and overexaggerate her name, annoyed she interrupted.

"Did you know that Elvis's eldest granddaughter is named Riley?"

"What?" I giggle. "Did you just bring up Elvis trivia on our date?

Jack buries his head in his hands, shielding his face. "Scratch that from the date record immediately. Please forget it."

I pull his hands off his face so I can see him. "Oh, come on. You're not here with her." I nod toward the flirty hostess. "You're here with me. I love strange trivia. Lay it on me."

"Nope. Not sexy," he says. I tickle his forearm, making my way slowly up his arm until he's holding back a grin.

"I'm not going to stop until you give me the strangest Elvis facts you got."

Jack inhales deeply. "He impersonated cops. He dyed his hair. He owned a chimp. He had a twin, and he hated fish," he says all in one breath, exhaling dramatically. Then he adds, "Oh, and he had a black belt, his karate name was Mr. Tiger."

"All right, the last fact was too much nerding-out, even for me," I tease. "It was a fun twenty-four hours of dating you, Jack Crawley, but I'll be taking my pizza to go."

"I knew you were going to end up breaking my heart, Walker." I watch his dimples grow more crooked the bigger his smile gets.

Our waitress brings the pizza, and we eat every last bite then go for a walk around the park.

"So, you've been on a date now, darlin'." He stops and turns to face me. "Other than the part where you tried to leave me. What do you think?"

I put my finger to my lip like I'm thinking hard. "It wasn't awful."

He clutches his chest like I've broken his heart. "Don't do me like that, Walker."

"I don't know." I grab his hands off his chest and hold them in mine. "I think I might like breaking into high schools and crashing country club parties more than dates." I take off playfully so he has to keep up with me. He catches me from behind and tickles my waist.

"So you want to live on the edge?" We stop in front of the blue Victorian where Hattie's School of Music is. He puts his back to the building and then leaps up high and grabs on to an old-fashioned fire escape. He pulls down the connecting ladder. "Let's go, girl. Show me what you got." He points to the rickety old ladder with an "I dare you" smile.

I'm drunk on him. I don't even think before I start to scale up to the second-story window. He follows close behind and leans over me so he can open the old window. I climb through first, and then he tumbles in behind me. We land in a small lesson room with a piano.

"We can't turn on the light. Hattie lives over that way." He points across town. "She'd notice it. But I don't think she can hear us." Jack starts tickling the piano keys.

I listen for a minute. "That's Beethoven."

"You remember," Jack says referring to our misadventure with Old Bo at the high school.

"Of course I do." I sit on the bench next to him and gently kiss his neck as he starts playing a new song. I should feel scandalized. Here I am breaking and entering again, but it feels perfect. "Can you play the *Doctor Who* theme song next?"

"The what?" Jack stops playing and looks perplexed. "Doctor What?"

"*Doctor Who*. The BBC show, you know dum dumm dummm dumm dum dum dum," I hum the iconic tune. "You were playing it on your violin the day we met when we were kids."

"Really?" Jack scratches his head. "I guess I must've heard it somewhere and gave it a try. I've never seen the show. I don't remember the song."

I stand up from the piano bench. "Jack Crawley. I asked you if you were a *Doctor Who* fan that day and you said 'yes.'"

"Of course, I said yes. When the prettiest girl you've ever seen asks you if you like something, you say 'yes.'"

I poke him in the chest with my finger and narrow my eyes. "So this whole thing between us is based on a lie."

He pulls me onto his lap, and I'm straddling him across the piano bench as he holds me tight. "I would do it all over again, Walker. Best lie I ever told."

Then he kisses me so passionately I forget all about the Doctor.

CHAPTER THIRTY-ONE

Wednesday, June 16th

I get up early for a jog and log my best mile yet at this altitude. I don't think my feet hit the pavement once. One date with Jack Crawley is like a steroid shot. After my shower, Margot and I walk to the Blue Ridge Roast, and Jack is working at the cash register when we arrive. He sees us but stays put at his post. We make our way to him to order our coffee, and somehow he seems even more handsome than he was the day before.

"Good morning, coffeehouse patrons," Jack says gregariously. "How can I help you on this fine day?" Without hesitation, I join Jack's silly game, because playful hijinks Jack is my all-time favorite version of him.

"We heard there was nice coffee, served by nice boys," I say and bat my eyelashes. Margot rolls her eyes.

"It's a shame I have a girlfriend," Jack says playfully. "Because I'd sure like to get your digits."

"Can we just order some damn coffee?" Margot interrupts our little game.

When Jack finally brings us our coffee, he delivers mine with a little peck on the cheek. Margot and I sit at our usual table and I look through the pages of my study guide, trying my best to focus on the practice questions about energy flow. But I can't stop peering up over the edge of the book to stare at Jack.

"Good Lord. You're a smitten kitten," Margot says as Andy sits down and joins the conversation.

"You must be off today," I say, looking him up and down. Instead of his uniform apron, he's wearing khaki shorts, a dri-fit t-shirt, and hiking boots.

"I'm supposed to be," he says. "Both Spencer and I were supposed to be off today and go for a hike, but he had a family thing in Knoxville at the last minute. I might as well clock in and work."

I look at the untouched practice quiz in my book. I'm never going to get anything done today with the devastatingly handsome man working a few feet away. "Leave your boots on. I'll go on a hike with you."

"Really? That could be kind of fun, Aves," he says. "Margot, you want to come with?"

She doesn't even answer. She points at the wedged heel on her boot as all the explanation he needs.

"How about Graybeard's?" I suggest. "I did it with Jack last winter. It was tough, but a lot of fun."

"No, Aves, not Graybeard's," Andy answers quickly. "I don't really like going up that hill. What about the West Ridge Trail?"

"Sounds good to me." I put my pencil in my book to mark my place and go to say bye to Jack.

"My girl and my best bro, I love it." Jack gives me a big kiss, then Andy and I head to his Saturn. After a quick stop at the cottage to grab better shoes, we're off on our hike.

It's not as challenging as Graybeard's but the sweeping views are equally as rewarding. When we reach a particularly peaceful overlook, Andy asks if we can stop. He sits on a rock and pulls his leatherbound sketchbook out of his satchel. We sit quietly together, and I watch him wield his magic on the paper, slowly creating a beautiful rendering of the tranquil valley below us.

"That's amazing," I say, wishing I could think of a more profound word to describe his art.

"Eh, I've done better," he says holding up the paper, scrutinizing it. "I've really gotten out of practice since I dropped out of art school. Chalkboards don't keep your skills up to par."

"Do you ever think about going back to school?" I ask.

He looks out over the valley and says wistfully, "Believe it or not, the option seems to be on the table right now. I might have a way to afford to enroll in the art program at UNC Asheville this fall, but I'm still thinking."

"Don't think too hard about it. You gotta follow your passion," I tell him.

"Wise words, kiddo." He ruffles my hair in a big brotherly gesture. It hurts my heart a little but feels good at the same time.

"Well, my brother's favorite movie was *Dead Poets Society*," I say. "If you watch that enough, you learn all the cheesy clichés."

"So, I guess that means I'll be living in an Elvis shrine," he says and stands to finish our hike.

"How's that?" I follow him down the trail.

"The last time we were having dinner at Della's, she offered me the spare room so I could save rent money and use it for tuition."

"You're going to be my boyfriend's roommate?" I ask playfully. "I guess that makes us in-laws of some sort."

We finish the hike, and Andy smiles as I campaign for him to take me to Paris someday when his work is inevitably on display at the Louvre.

CHAPTER THIRTY-TWO

Friday, July 1ˢᵗ

It's hot as hell in Black Mountain, but I don't bother to go home and shower after my morning run. I'm so addicted to Jack I can't wait an extra hour to see him. So, instead of ending my morning route at the cottage, I finish it at Blue Ridge Roast and shamelessly give Jack and Andy sweaty hugs before I settle into my green velvet chair. I pull out my phone and start to mindlessly scroll when I spot Jack out of the corner of my eye. He's standing behind the counter quietly waving his hands, trying to get my attention. My legs are a little sore from the run, but I hurry across the café to the counter to see what the fuss is about.

"Avery, Avery." Jack is so excited about something he can barely get his words out. "Look at her." He nods toward a college-aged girl who looks way too put together for this early in the morning. She has on a flowy summer dress, blown-out hair, and flawless skin. "Don't be so obvious, Walker."

"What? You told me to look at her." I give him an incredulous look.

"Shhhh." Jack is downright giddy. "She ordered coffee."

"Okay, that's what most people do in a coffeehouse." I lean against the counter so we can whisper.

"Let me finish." He holds up the cup he's written her order and name on. "Look. Look at her name. It's Olivia-Catherine."

It takes me a minute, and then I realize what he's talking about. Olivia-Catherine. O.C. My excitement level immediately matches his. "Oh my god. What do we do?"

"I don't know, but we have to do something, right?" he whispers.

I take a deep breath so I can think straight. "Step one. Make her coffee."

"Right."

"Step two. When you give it to her, talk to her a little, get to know her, see if she fits the profile."

"How do I do that?" he asks.

"Come on, man." I hiss. "You're Jack Crawley. Charm her. It's what you do." He nods and starts making her coffee.

When he finishes and calls Olivia-Catherine to the counter, I stand right there so I can hear everything.

"So, you live around here?" Jack asks. I cringe a little. Come on, Jack. Charming, not creepy.

Olivia-Catherine shakes her head and starts to walk away. I don't blame her. I would do the same thing. He comes around the counter before she can get out the door.

"You have such a pretty name," he says.

"Thanks," Olivia-Catherine answers. She isn't charmed.

"I'm wondering what type of last name a girl with such a pretty first name might have." Too far Jack. O.C. is now thoroughly creeped out and pushes past Jack to get the heck out of the Blue Ridge Roast. I feel like I am watching the one thread still tying me to my brother snap in two. A sense of urgency washes over me, and without thinking I run out the door and chase O.C. down the street.

"Hey," I shout until she stops. "I'm so sorry about the guy in the coffee shop. Please don't be mad, but I told him to ask you those stupid questions."

She stops and listens, looking me up and down, trying to decide if I'm a dangerous crazy person or a run-of-the-mill crazy person. But she doesn't leave, so I keep talking.

"Listen, I know this is going to sound really strange, but my brother passed away last fall. After he died, I found out he had had a really close friend in Black Mountain, and her name might be something like Olivia-Catherine." I take a deep breath, knowing everything could change depending on how she answers the next question. "Did you ever know somebody named Whit Walker?"

Olivia-Catherine looks me straight in the eye and takes her time before she says, "No, sweetheart. I've never known anybody with that name."

"Okay, well, thanks for listening." O.C. waves good-bye politely and walks away.

I head back into the coffeehouse with my head hung low. Jack greets me with a big hug. I know he can tell from my face I didn't get the answer I'd hoped for. He kisses the top of my head and promises he'll take a break as soon as he can.

When the morning rush is over, Jack and Andy come and sit with me. I expect them to start comforting me, but the conversation takes a different direction.

"Avery, this whole thing has gone too far," Andy says in a serious tone. "You and Jack literally chased a paying customer out of the coffeehouse. I know I'm your friend, but I'm also the manager here." Andy pauses to make sure I'm not crying or anything, then he continues. "You guys aren't going to find who you are looking for, and obsessing over it makes you both act crazy. I think you need to put this to rest. I know it sucks, but you need to move on."

Jack puts a protective arm around me. "Dude, that's way too harsh. Come on."

"Aves," Andy softens his tone and gently puts his hand on my shoulder. "When you first told me about this, you told me you wanted to figure out who OCMC was so you could tell her Whit died so she wasn't walking around wondering why he ghosted her. Don't you think she's probably Googled him by now? If she did, she would've found his obituary. If that's really the reason why you were doing it, then you don't need to feel like you failed. I'm sure she knows by now."

I sink into the green velvet chair and think hard about what Andy said. He isn't wrong. The situation felt so urgent last winter because I wanted OCMC to know what happened to Whit, to not remember him as a jerk. But surely Whit wouldn't've fallen in love with a dimwit. She would've been smart enough to know something wasn't right and do her research.

I nod but stay quiet because the truth is, even if Andy is kind of right, something still feels off. Why did she block Whit's number? Why did she cut off her own number? What is she hiding? If she found his obit, why wouldn't she get in touch with my family?

"You make some good points," I say. "Maybe we should take a little break from all the madness, Detective Crawley?"

"Is that really what you want?" Jack asks, looking puzzled.

"For now," I mutter. I feel more confused than the day we unlocked Whit's phone. I'm really not sure what I want.

When Jack gets off work that night, he comes to the cottage to check on me, and we hang out on Gran's screened porch. We sit on the white metal glider my grandparents have had since the seventies. I put my head in Jack's lap and look up at him while he plays with my hair.

"Did Andy hurt your feelings today?"

"No. I'm not nearly as delicate as you think I am." I listen to my own words as they leave my mouth, and I know I need to tell Jack some news I've been sitting on for a few days. I lift my head off his lap and sit up. "I need to tell you something you might not like."

"I like everything you tell me," Jack says, flirting. "Try me."

I pull away from him a little on the glider and look off at the mountains as I deliver the news. "Gran offered to take me and Margot to Boston next week to tour Boston University." It's no secret that Gran will be the one footing the bill for my college, so she also wants to be the one to check it out with me.

"That's great." Jack smiles big, so I know he doesn't get what I'm saying. "Badass Avery headed to the Ivy leagues."

"BU isn't the Ivy leagues." I correct him, avoiding the downside to this news. "We're going to stay a whole week and do some tourist stuff. Maybe check out Tufts and MIT too. I'm only here for a few more weeks. I hate to lose so much time with you."

Jack's face drops a little, then he looks over his shoulder to see if Gran is watching us from the kitchen window, then leans in and kisses me.

I put my hands on his face and kiss him back, then pull away. "You're not mad?"

"I'm sad, but it's not like it's good-bye. You'll be back. We still have time." He takes my hand off his cheek and plays with my fingers. "Besides, even after you head back to Nashville, I'm going to call you every day, and I'm going to visit you if I have to hitchhike the whole way."

The word "good-bye" makes me want to cry, so I change the subject. "It's Friday. Are we going on a date tonight?"

"Do you want romance or hijinks?" Jack asks, his crooked dimples looking extra charming in the afternoon light.

I raise my eyebrows. "Can't we do both?"

"God, I'm going to miss you next week, Avery Jane Walker." Jack pops up from the glider and claps his hands. "I've got it."

He looks at his watch. "All right. If we're going to do this you've got to go get changed, and we need to walk fast to make it before dark."

I hop up. "Give me five minutes. I'll be right back."

"Wait, don't dress up. Put on like an old t-shirt, something that can get wet."

"Wet?"

"Trust me."

"You're lucky you're cute."

I toss on a WPA t-shirt and pair of running shorts then knot my hair into a tight braid to protect it from whatever "wet" means.

"Gran, I'm going out with Jack. I'll be home before curfew, promise." I give Gran a quick hug and find Jack waiting on the porch with a big grin, ready to go.

"Let's do this, Walker."

CHAPTER THIRTY-THREE

We walk quickly, racing the sun, to the west side of town. We reach a road I've never been down before. "It's like ten minutes down this street," Jack says and leads me by the hand.

Eventually, the road turns into a bridge, and he tells me we've reached our date. He points to the river, then takes off his shirt and stands on the rail of the bridge. "Water looks plenty deep. C'mon up, Walker."

"Are you serious?" I shout. He gives me a charming, full-dimple grin, and reaches a hand out to help me up.

"I'll hold your hand the whole time," he says. "Don't look down before we jump."

I climb up quickly, expecting to freak out the moment I'm up there, but to my surprise I'm not even a little scared. We are standing together on the ledge of a bridge over a mountain river, and I am actually excited to take the plunge.

"Let's do it," I say. He seems shocked when I'm the one who initiates the jump. We fall through the air, tightly squeezing each other's hand until we hit the freezing cold river. We come up from under the water, laughing and kissing, and swim to the riverbank.

"That was amazing," I scream as loud as I can into the gully.

"You're amazing," Jack says and kisses me hard.

We sit on a big rock and drip dry in each other's arms, talking about everything and nothing. We watch the sun go down over the bridge, then start to walk back to his house. We're about halfway there when the dark sky lights up with a huge streak of lightning. His hand squeezes mine tight. "It's only heat lightning. You don't need to be scared," I say. But as soon as the words leave my mouth a huge thunderclap fills the air.

"You ready to run, Walker?" he asks, and we both take off sprinting up the mountain. "You're too slow. We aren't going to make it."

"Cross-country is about endurance, not speed," I say in my defense.

He stops and bends down so I can hop on his back, then he carries me up the hill like he's saving me from a wildfire, instead of a mild thunderstorm. Big fat raindrops start falling right as we reach Oakley Road. When we reach the bottom of Jack's stone steps, he bends down, and I hop off his back. He starts kissing me deeply, and intense. He stops to say something, but now the rain is so loud I can't hear him.

"I never understood why the movies make kissing in the rain look romantic," I shout. "It's really cold, and way too loud."

"Let's go inside and dry off," he shouts back. Then he lifts me, I wrap my legs around his waist, and he carries me to his room. Of course, I've been to Jack Crawley's room before, but I've never been to Jack Crawley's room like this.

"I'm freezing," I say as he sets me down on his bed and shuts the door behind us.

"Then you need to get out of those wet clothes," he retorts quickly. I can tell he's being silly, but I still throw a pillow at him and say, "Is that the best line you have?"

He goes to his drawer and pulls out a big t-shirt and a pair of gym shorts, and then tosses them to me. "I'll turn around while you change. It won't be easy, but I'll do it." He puts his hands over his eyes, but peeks through the fingers.

I throw another pillow at him and go to the hall bathroom.

170

I pull my phone out of my bag, and I'm thankful to see it stayed mostly dry, but I'm supremely disappointed when I see what time it is. Shit. It's already 11:00.

I feel sick to my stomach thinking about saying good-bye to Jack. I put on the shirt and gym shorts, and I look comical. But when I walk into his room, Jack doesn't think so.

"God, you're sexy, Walker," he says and starts kissing me again.

I pull away. "I have to go home soon."

"But it's storming out." He looks genuinely concerned. "I'd be scared to death if I knew you were walking home through that."

My phone is still in my hand, and before I can think too hard about it, I'm typing out a text to Margot.

Me: Are you home?

Margot: Yes.

Me: Can you cover for me with Gran? Act like I'm already asleep or something.

Margot sends a long strand of winking mojos, peaches, and eggplants back to me. Even though I don't like Margot's insinuation, I'm so relieved I don't have to say good-bye to Jack yet. I put down the phone and wrap my hands around his neck. "I'm not going anywhere."

He carries me to his bed, and lays me down, kissing my neck and my earlobe. It feels amazing and scary. I would do anything for Jack, and that terrifies me.

I pull his face up to mine and brush away a strand of his long black hair before I kiss him deeply, open-mouthed. We start kissing more passionately than we ever have before. His hands slowly explore my body, and mine slowly explore his. Things keep progressing, but when I pull the t-shirt he loaned me over my head, tossing it to the floor, he pulls back away from me.

"Are you okay?" His voice is raspy and breathy. "We don't need to do anything you don't want to do."

"I know."

"I mean it's not like I don't want to... I mean god, you're beautiful, and you're in my bed, and I want to, but I only want to if you want to." He's nervous and more vulnerable than I've ever seen him.

I put my hand on his bare chest to calm him down. "Can I be honest? It kind of freaks me out you're a lot more experienced than I am. Like a lot."

He laughs and pulls the hand on his chest up to his lips, kissing my fingers tenderly. "That whole bad boy, ladies' man, musician thing is an illusion, you know that, right? You'd be my first too."

It's my turn to laugh. "I don't believe you for a minute."

"Come on, I've been hung up on you since I was thirteen years old. There's never been anybody but you. You're everything to me, and always have been."

I wrap my hands around the back of his neck and start kissing him deeply and urgently, feeling my way across every sexy muscle of his body.

I really want to do this right because I think there's something romantic and poetic about being each other's first kisses and each other's first for the big stuff.

But Jack slows things down, and we cuddle, then we end up falling asleep in each other's arms.

CHAPTER THIRTY-FOUR

Saturday, July 2ⁿᵈ

I wake up with my head nestled in the nook between Jack's shoulder and his chest. I lift my head and softly kiss Jack's lips. He stirs and wakes, then takes a deep breath. "My pillows smell like coconut and sunshine now."

He reaches for his phone on the nightstand and sees the time. "You gotta go, I don't want to get you in trouble," he says, but each punctuated with a kiss. I pull on my shoes, and he helps me out his bedroom window, squeezing me around the waist and burying his head into my back as I go. The sun isn't up as I sneak back to the cottage, and Gran seems none the wiser I never came home last night.

"Are you all packed for our big trip tomorrow, Avery?" Gran asks over breakfast. "If you are, I was hoping you could pencil your dear grandmother into your schedule for some cards later."

"I'm sure she's too busy with her townie-freak boyfriend," Margot says.

"Not true," I say as I grab a second breakfast roll out of the basket. "Jack, my non-townie-freak boyfriend, is working all day. I'm going to go say hi before his shift starts this morning, and then I'll be right home. Maybe we can play speed solitaire, Gran?"

"Kiss-ass," Margot whispers. I let her comment slide because after last night I feel nothing but rainbows and sunshine today.

When I arrive at the café, Jack is already sitting on the bench out front with a blueberry bagel with extra cream cheese waiting for me. I don't care I've eaten two sweet rolls with Gran. I take it from him, so smitten my boyfriend is not only stone-cold hot but thoughtful too.

"Good morning, beautiful," he says with a full-teeth grin.

Eating a bagel with extra cream cheese is challenging with only one hand, but I do it because I don't want to let go of Jack's hand even for a second.

He leans in until our foreheads are touching. "Do you really have to go all the way to Boston for college?" he asks. "There are plenty of science nerd schools in North Carolina. Why can't you go to Duke or Chapel Hill?"

"Boston University is my dream," I say. "They have the best neuroscience and sports brain injury program in the country." He tightens his upper lip. "Plus the brownstones, the town, the whole vibe," I say dreamily. "You get it, right?"

"Of course I don't get it." He pulls his forehead away from mine. "I'm not even going to college."

"I am sorry, what?" How is it possible we've never talked about this before? "Why wouldn't you go to college?"

"I told you I barely attend classes." Then he points out at the town square. "Plus, have you honestly not noticed I'm poor? It's not like I'm some sort of secret genius either. Della will be thrilled if I manage to graduate high school."

"You're such a gifted musician," I say gently.

There's a moment of quiet between us before I sit up straight excited. "Why didn't I think of this before? You should apply to Berklee College of Music in Boston. We could be together there, both of us doing our thing. It would be so amazing."

"Did you listen to anything I said?" He's angry in a way I've never seen them before. "I am poor. I have bad grades. I'm not going to any college, let alone one in Boston."

"Well then, what will you do after you graduate?"

"I'll probably pick up more shifts at Blue Ridge Roast." He shrugs and then he looks less angry but sadder.

"But you're so amazing and talented. You could be so much more than this." I point at the coffee shop. As soon as the words leave my mouth, I regret them.

"You don't get it." He stands and the anger is back. "Look, the only thing we ever had in common is looking for OCMC. We quit that, so now there really isn't anything else between us."

"But I care about you so much, and I know you care about me too." I can feel the tears welling up in my eyes, and I try to choke them back.

"Avery, I'm a poor kid from a poor mountain town. You are a rich kid who vacations here." He's pacing. "You know how kissing in the rain is only romantic in the movies?"

I nod.

"Rich kids and poor kids only work in the movies, not in real life." He continues to pace. "I've wanted you to be my girlfriend since I was thirteen, but not like this."

"What are you saying?" I grab his arm and make him look at me.

"I'm saying that I'm not good enough for you, and nothing can ever change that. You care so much about being perfect for your parents and your gran. If you're going to keep being little Miss Perfect, we both know you need to be with somebody better than me. I'm never going to be good enough."

"That is such a low blow. My parents just lost a child. Making their lives easier isn't some random choice, it's what I have to do." I can feel the physical pain in my chest. It's the first time I get why it's called heartache.

"That's bullshit. You are living in some fantasy of a perfect little life," he says. "Our worlds are too different, princess."

The word "princess" gouges my soul. He can be such an asshole. I have nothing left to say if he's going to resort to name-calling. I sit quietly, stewing, waiting for an apology, but it doesn't come.

"When you get back from Boston, I think we should be friends again. It makes more sense." He walks into Blue Ridge Roast without turning to look back at me.

During the walk back to the cottage, I remind myself over and over this is what Jack does. He defaults to asshole when he's overwhelmed. He did it the first night we met at the bonfire. He did it after our hike to Graybeard's. He's doing it again. Tonight there will be an email, or a note wrapped around a rock, or a knock on the door. He'll apologize for blowing up and beg to get back together.

As Gran and I play speed solitaire on the porch, I keep repeating this refrain in my head. He defaults to being an asshole, but he's still Jack. He'll come around.

I don't sleep at all. It reminds me of the first few nights during Christmas break. I keep my gaze trained on the window, half expecting him to appear at the sliding glass door any minute to tell me he didn't mean what he said. At some point I drift off, but wake up suddenly, checking my email for the apology note, but it's not there.

In the morning there's no rock or symbolic gesture under the windshield wiper.

I keep thinking he'll show up.

He has to show up.

How can he kiss me so passionately one day, and break up with me the next?

Our flight is early, and the limo is pulling out of the gravel driveway at 7 a.m.

No sign of Jack.

No sign of the boy in whose bed I was sleeping with my head cuddled in his nook yesterday morning.

CHAPTER THIRTY-FIVE

Sunday, July 3rd

Margot, Gran, and I land in Boston before noon. As soon as the plane hits the ground, I turn on my phone, expecting to see missed calls and texts from Violin-Jack. But my home screen is hauntingly blank. I open up my text stream and feel pain in my chest when I read the last text Jack sent me. It's from early Saturday morning.

Violin-Jack: Did ya get home safe, Walker? I miss you already.

During the cab ride to our hotel, I fiddle with my phone, willing it to ring or beep with a text. As we exit the taxi, Margot grabs my arm and pulls me out of Gran's earshot. "Girl, I'm sorry your townie broke your heart, but you gotta put the phone down and look around. You need to figure out if you want to live in this city for the next four years. Focus."

She's right. I tuck my phone into my KAVU bag, vowing to leave it there unless I actually need it. We check into the Hilton overlooking Boston Common, and Gran announces she needs to rest. Margot and I are itching to get out and explore, so we freshen up and study a map of the T on Margot's phone.

It's my first time in Boston, and I am hoping to fall in love with the city as much as I fell in love with the pictures on BU's website.

Margot and I take the Green Line to Boston University's campus and wander around, taking it all in. It's fun to see the campus without an official tour guide. Margot is only weeks away from being a college student, and with her by my side, we blend in with the summer session students.

We walk through the quad, admire the brownstone along Bay Street, and watch the students, most of whom are in glasses with oversize backpacks. I can't picture Jack here in his work boots and unironically ripped jeans.

Margot and I grab a coffee and a table by the window in the Pavement Coffeehouse on campus. I notice that the barista who makes our drinks has on a tight vee-neck t-shirt, skinny jeans, and some sort of tribal hair wrap around his white dude dreadlocks. A far cry from the employees of Blue Ridge Roast.

I'm looking out the window thinking about everything Jack said. Maybe he wasn't defaulting to an asshole. Maybe he was telling it like it is.

Our lives are headed in different directions. I'm an aspiring scientist, damn it. Surely, I should understand I wasn't actually falling in love. Clearly, my teenage hormones were releasing increased oxytocin and creating changes in the biochemistry of my brain. That's neuroscience, not romance.

The next day, the fourth of July, the campus is closed, so we spend the day doing patriotic things like walking the Freedom Trail and visiting Paul Revere's grave. In the evening we watch the fireworks over the Charles River from our hotel balcony. Every bright boom in the air makes me think, "Jack who?"

I only have one love now, and it's Boston.

On Wednesday we do the formal campus tour with Gran, and the biochemistry in my brain falls even more in love with every little aspect of the campus, right down to the geometric patterns on the floors of the cutting-edge science labs.

After the college business is out of the way, we spend the next few days doing touristy things in Boston: Faneuil Hall, eating cannolis in the North End, and shopping on Newbury Street. I log some epic runs through Boston Common and along the Charles River. All the while, my phone stays tucked in my bag, only vibrating for the occasional group text from Mom and Dad asking for pictures and updates.

Nothing from Jack.

On our last afternoon in town, one of Gran's church friends from Charlotte calls and insists we try Borders Café for a delicious Mexican lunch. Mexican food sounds good, so we hop on the Red Line and cross the Charles River, exiting the T at Harvard Square.

We follow the brick sidewalks of Cambridge to Borders Café and settle into a table Gran approves of. She's the pickiest restaurant patron alive. She can't be too close to the kitchen, and heaven forbid she feels a draft from the front entrance. I'm starting to browse the menu when I hear a male voice shout, "Avery Walker," from the other side of the restaurant.

"Of all the Mexican restaurants in all of Boston," Henry Warden says, standing side by side with his older brother, Matt.

"What are the chances?" I stand from our table and give him a restrained side hug. I'm not sure exactly how I'm supposed to greet him after blowing him off after prom. Seriously, what are the chances? "Gran, Margot, this is my friend Henry and his brother Matt who goes to school here."

"Of course, of course," Gran swoons. "I recognize you from Avery's prom pictures. You were quite handsome in your tuxedo. You must join us. There's plenty of room."

"Gran, I'm sure they don't want to." My argument is lost over the sound of moving chairs, and making space for the Warden brothers to join our party.

"So how do you like Harvard, Matt?" Margot dives right into flirting shamelessly, batting her long black eyelashes and leaning into him like he's the most fascinating guy in the world.

"It's all right. Can't complain about the local restaurant scene." Matt picks up his menu and smiles at Margot, seemingly charmed by her flirting.

"I can't imagine Boston in the winter," Margot says. "That's why I'm going to the University of Miami. Bikinis every day." I narrow my eyes at her, willing her to tone it down before she catches hell from Gran.

"Where are you going to school, Henry?" Gran asks, clearly trying to divert the conversation from Margot's bikinis.

"I'm hoping to go to Harvard with my brother next year. That's why I'm visiting, ma'am," he half stutters. "If I get in, of course."

As the conversation continues, Gran is practically drooling every time the word "Harvard" comes out of one of the Warden brothers' mouths. At one point, Margot leans over and whispers in my ear, "Good Lord. Gran needs to go take a cold shower." As I watch the scene around the table, I can't help but remember the way Gran looked at Della's beat-up blue truck. It's impossible to picture Jack sitting around this lunch table with this group.

As we talk, it's easy to remember why I spent so much of the spring semester in the library with Henry. He's easy to talk to and handles himself well with my overbearing Gran.

"Have you ever been to the Blue Ridge Mountains, Henry?" Gran asks between bites of her taco salad.

"No, ma'am. I don't believe I have," he answers politely. "Our family always vacations at the beach."

"Well, you simply must come to visit Black Mountain with Avery sometime," Gran says. "It's only a six-hour drive from Nashville, and we have a spare room." I smile and nod because anything else would be rude.

Margot whispers in my ear, "That oughta be good," then makes a devious, evil-plot, gesture with her hands. She then shifts her attention back toward Matt, and I don't think either of them takes their eyes off each other for the rest of lunch.

"Do you ladies want to go for a walk around campus with us?" Matt asks as we leave the restaurant. "I can give you an unofficial tour."

"They would love that," Gran answers on our behalf. "I'll take a cab back to the hotel. You all take your time."

Matt's "unofficial campus tour" leads us straight to his dorm room where he wastes no time offering Margot a drink. The two of them sit on his loft bed, red solo cups in hand, heads close together, deeply engaged in conversation.

Henry and I hang out on the musty futon in the common room lounge of Matt's building. I expect Henry to be shy and timid, but campus life suits him. He sits comfortably with one arm resting on the back of the futon, a beer bottle in the other hand, asking all about my summer.

I talk about hiking and going to Dollywood, and Henry shares summer stories of his own, but I barely listen. Is sitting on this futon with Henry wrong? I guess I don't technically have a boyfriend anymore, even if my heart hasn't accepted it.

After Henry finishes his beer, he seems to gain some extra liquid courage. "Can I ask you something?"

"Sure."

"Why did you run away from me after prom? I kind of thought maybe you liked me. Was I totally wrong?"

I don't want to have this conversation. "You weren't totally wrong." I bite the inside of my cheek and stare at the checkered pattern of the linoleum floor. "Um, if you get another beer, could you get me one too?"

He leaps up from the futon like a rocket and quickly returns with two beers, handing me one. I take a sip, and it's as gross as I imagined it would be, but it does do the trick of loosening my tongue. As I peel at the label, I tell Henry everything. How I knew Jack could be a jerk and a rebel, but I fell for him anyway. How I thought we were falling in love, but now I don't know. How Jack thinks I need everyone to believe I'm perfect.

Henry listens carefully then says, "You deserve better than that." He takes a deep breath, and then a big sip of beer. "Think about how great it would be if we were both here in Boston next fall." I take a long, hard look at Henry. His professor-esque good looks, his impressive resumé, his college choice—which happens to be a quick

T ride away from BU—and it's sort of cruel, but he's not Jack. And that includes all the things about Jack, especially the ease with which he broke up with me and didn't seem to give it another thought.

My mind plays a slideshow of one version of my senior year in high school: flirtatious study sessions for AP tests, visits to Make-Out Mountain, opening our college acceptance emails together, and my parents beaming proudly while their daughter's boyfriend gives his valedictory speech at graduation. Love is only the release of chemicals in our brain. I could make this work.

I set my beer bottle on the linoleum floor and shift my body a little closer to Henry's. Our gazes meet, then our lips.

Kissing Henry is different from kissing Jack. It's polite. No passion, and it doesn't make my heart thunder against my rib cage. But it feels pleasant, and it makes a lot more sense.

Margot, Gran, and I leave Boston the next day, and when we land at the Asheville airport, I turn on my phone to a bevy of sweet sentiments from Henry. Nothing from Jack. As our town car pulls up to the cottage, I can see through the trees there's a big vehicle parked down the driveway. My heart is in my throat, hoping as the car comes into focus it's an old blue truck. It has to be.

But it's not.

As soon as we hit the driveway, I recognize the Walker Family Yukon parked in front of Huckleberry Cottage. Mom and Dad are standing on the front porch waving anxiously.

"Welcome back from the big city, kiddo," Dad shouts. His arm is around Mom, and he looks almost happy. His eyes still don't have the cheesy dad twinkle they used to, but at least they seem more focused and alert.

"I hope you don't mind us crashing your summer vacation," Mom says, pulling me in for a hug. "We missed you too much."

We all sit on the screened-in porch, and I tell Mom and Dad how amazing Boston is.

"Are we going to get to meet your beau while we are here?" Dad asks when the college talk winds down. Margot gives me a worried look like she thinks I'm going to burst into tears or something.

"Probably not," I say, avoiding eye contact with Margot. "We weren't really serious, and things kind of fizzled out."

"Then maybe you'll think about coming home early with us," Mom says. "The house is too quiet without you. We miss you."

I'm supposed to be in Black Mountain for two more weeks, and I should probably head back to Nashville now. I'm not even thinking about Jack as I weigh my options. I'm thinking about Whit and OCMC.

The only progress I've made this summer was crossing a single stranger, Olivia-Catherine, off the possible suspect lists. I'm not ready to give up. It's still important to me, but Black Mountain feels full of nothing but dead ends.

Maybe a better option would be to go home and focus my attention on Whit instead of OCMC. It's not like I have anybody here to help me. Margot is bored with it all. Andy thinks it's creepy, and Jack… I have no clue what Jack thinks about anything anymore.

I'm mulling all of this over when my phone vibrates in my hand.

Henry Warden: I miss you, how many more days until you're back in Nashville?

I put my phone down and look at Mom and Dad, holding hands like they used to do.

"I'm ready," I say. "Let's go home."

CHAPTER THIRTY-SIX

Tuesday, July 11th

Mom, Dad, and I are loaded up in the Walker Family Yukon and we're heading down Interstate 40, back to Nashville. During my last few days in Black Mountain, I said my good-byes to Andy, Spencer, and Della, strategically picking times and places when and where I knew Jack wouldn't be around. Margot and I cried and hugged on the front porch before I left. We made a vow to keep "Cousin Camp" alive even though we're practically grown-ups. Margot is the closest thing to a living sibling I'll ever have now, and I don't want to let that go. I promised her to always meet up at Huckleberry Cottage, anytime I can.

Once we arrive home, I text Henry and ask if he wants to catch a movie. When he arrives to pick me up, he has a gift for me carefully wrapped in red and black paper. I invite him inside because there is nothing about Henry I need to hide for my parents' sake. I unwrap the gift, and it's a cute little stuffed terrier: the Boston University mascot wearing a BU hoodie.

"I picked it up before I left Boston last week," he says. "I know you're going to get into BU." I give him a hug, and a short, closed-mouth kiss on the lips. Before we leave for the movies, I take the little stuffed dog up to my room and set it on my nightstand, next to the WW rock.

***

By the time senior year starts at WP, Henry and I are officially boyfriend and girlfriend. We tell Riley our relationship status at the back-to-school senior BBQ. She acts thrilled and squeals "double dates." But when we get home, she follows me up to my room, sits on my bed, and her expression becomes serious.

"Are you really over Jack?" she asks.

"Of course not," I answer honestly because it's Riley, and she would know if I were lying. "But it never really made sense between us. Henry's better for me. You think we're good together, right?"

"Of course. If there was an Advanced Placement category for Homecoming Queen and King, you and Henry would win hands down." Riley laughs at her joke. "But I keep thinking about Dollywood."

"Speaking of Advanced Placement, let me see your schedule for the fall semester," I say, changing the subject. I know I won't be able to bounce back if I allow myself to think about Dollywood.

Riley pulls up her class schedule on her glittery pink phone and hands it to me, as I hand her mine. We analyze our schedules and who's in what sections of what AP classes. When it's time for her to go meet up with Will, she hands me my phone, and out of habit, I click on my inbox as soon as it's in my hands.

It's as if somehow Jack knew Riley and I were talking about him. After a whole month of complete radio silence, his name is sitting in my inbox.

Subject: *Can we be pen pals again?*

And then, all the body of the email says is ***"Yours, Jack."***

I'm not sure how I'm supposed to feel when I'm content with my new boyfriend, and my ex emails me out of the blue.

I can't hide my smile when I see the name Jack on my screen. Boyfriend, or only a long-distance friend, the truth is I miss Jack Crawley terribly. This is the longest we've ever gone without talking to each other since that night at the bonfire last Christmas.

I consider playing it cool and waiting a week or two to reply, but I don't. I genuinely hate not knowing what's going on in his life.

Subject: Can we be pen pals again?

Jack,

I'd like to be your pen pal again. Actually, I owe you a "thank you." I took the SAT II subject test last week, and I'm pretty sure I nailed it. So thanks for providing me with the comfy green velvet chair to study in all summer.

Your pen pal,

Avery

Avery,

I'm so happy to hear from you, and I'm glad all those hours studying paid off. Amazing. So much to tell you. A lot has changed since you left. A new owner bought the Blue Ridge Roast, and he is trying to turn it into a coffeehouse/open mic type vibe. Guess who he has playing sets every Friday and Saturday night? Hope you get to come and see some time. You would love it. He's been good to Andy letting him do art for the new menus. Things are looking up around here.

How are you? How's Margot and how's Riley? How are your parents?

Don't be a stranger.

Your pen pal,

Jack

I can't answer his last question. Every tiny amount of normalcy that returned between my parents over the summer has all but disappeared as football season rears its ugly head.

It makes me think about a book I read on neuropsychology about when Amish teenagers take a Rumspringa. You'd think they'd go wild being free from all the routines and restrictions, but neurobiology doesn't allow for that. More than ninety percent of Amish teens return to the Amish community from Rumspringa because they don't know what to do without the pillars their lives were built around.

That's how Mom, Dad, and I feel about football. We have no joy in finally having freedom on Friday nights. We're lost without the diets, the practices, and the game-day rituals.

But unlike the Amish, for the Walkers there's no community to return to.

The pillar our family was built around is gone forever.

***

We survive the quiet Friday nights of September, but when the calendar flips to October, all three of us struggle knowing the first anniversary of Whit's death is quickly approaching. Especially me. I had a whole year to figure out who OCMC is and I completely failed. But my one saving grace is my Black Mountain friend crew manage to overturn a Dead Sibling Society Rule. Unlike the kids at Warner Prep, they aren't afraid to talk to me about Whit, and death, and all the shitty things.

Jack emails me often, choosing measured words managing to be platonic and deeply caring.

Avery,

Think about you every time the football team at BMHS wears their uniforms to school. (Yes, I've actually been showing up at school. You'd be so proud.) I know it must be hard to see all the Warner Prep uniforms in the hallways. I'm so sorry.

Your pen pal,

Jack

Andy checks in via text.

BlueRidgeAndy: Hey Aves, want you to know, I'm here if you ever want to talk.

Margot calls me almost every day. "Don't get me wrong, I love South Beach," Margot says from her dorm room, which sounds like it has at least eight noisy co-eds crammed into the tiny space. "But I miss the leaves and the pumpkin spice lattes, you know? Do you want me to visit you this fall?"

Riley is always willing to hide with me in the girls' locker room during football pep rallies. And Henry is the picture-perfect boyfriend. He comes over every Friday night to play board games with me and my parents. It helps us get our mind off football, and Henry doesn't mind because he doesn't follow football anyway.

The Warner Prep football field without number eight feels like a grandmother without clothes on. It's nauseating and none of us even want to picture it.

***

The second Friday in October, Mom makes pork chops and peas, and I know she must be planning a Walker family chat.

When we're all at the table, Dad says, "Avery, Mom and I can't stand the thought of being in this house next week when Whit's anniversary rolls around."

"I know how you feel." I give them sympathetic looks.

"Margot called," Mom says. "Next week is her fall break. She offered to fly home and meet us at Huckleberry Cottage, so we can get away from here. I know you'd have to miss a cross-country meet to leave town next weekend, but…"

I interrupt her. "I'm in, Mom. I'd rather be anywhere but here."

I've never been to Black Mountain in the fall. I've never actually been anywhere in the fall except football fields. I think about the framed picture of Gran and Grandpa Tom hanging in the entryway of the cottage with the vibrant autumn leaves shining in the background. The mountains in the fall sound nice. Seeing Margot and anybody else from Black Mountain sounds nice too.

When I leave the table, I go upstairs and pull Whit's phone out of my nightstand for the first time in a long time. I reread his texts for the millionth time, willing something to jump out at me.

Next weekend will be exactly a year since the last time Whit texted OCMC. I bet she's dreading the anniversary too.

I'm so mad at myself for not finding her. She belongs with my family this weekend. I wish she could sit with us on the screened porch of the cottage and reminisce about Whit alongside the other people who loved him.

I look across the hallway at Whit's bedroom door and whisper, "I'm so sorry I didn't find her, Whit."

CHAPTER THIRTY-SEVEN

Wednesday, October 19th

Mom and Dad let me skip school so our trip can overlap with Margot's fall break. We all arrive at Huckleberry Cottage on Wednesday. Our first afternoon there we sit in the screened-in porch and make small talk with Gran. I keep waiting for somebody to bring up an excuse to go into town. Does Gran need butter? Does Margot want to go for a run? C'mon. Somebody needs to give me an excuse to go by the Blue Ridge Roast.

I'm not excited to see Jack, but he knows I'm here, and I know he works most afternoons after school. I'm sure he's watching the door of the café. I imagine seeing him will be awkward, but that's the thing with Jack, he knows how to charm all the awkward out of a room. I want to stop worrying about seeing him, and have it behind me.

Finally Margot says, "Hey, Avery, you look tired. Should we go get some coffee?"

"Stay clear of the Blue Ridge Roast, Avery," Gran says. "That local Jack fellow still works there. I saw him taking out the trash the other day." She makes a disgusted face and it's clear she's still horrified I ever dated a person who works such a lowly job where one touches garbage.

Gran practically has me betrothed to Henry. If it were socially acceptable to draw up a contract and make Henry sign on the dotted line, Gran would do it in a heartbeat.

"Yes, ma'am," I say as I grab my purse and put on a cute pair of tall brown boots. As we walk down the driveway, Margot says, "I mean we are still going to the Blue Ridge, right?"

"Do I really have to answer?" I loop my arm through hers as we walk. "I want to see Andy, you know."

"Right," Margot says with a sarcastic laugh. "So, what's going to happen between you and Jack this week?

"Margot," I say, horrified, as we keep walking. "I have a boyfriend. I have Henry. Jack and I dated for barely a month. We were friends before and we're friends now. Nothing more to be said."

"Is Jack on the same page?" she asks as we reach the door of Blue Ridge Roast. "I mean did y'all talk about it or anything?"

"Of course we're on the same page." I pause at the door, but I don't answer the second part of Margot's question because the truth is in all the emails we've exchanged the past few weeks, we've completely avoided the topic of "us."

We go inside, and Jack's behind the counter taking a customer's order. I can't help but notice he's a little buff-er, and maybe a little more ruggedly handsome than I remember. And those dimples. How did I manage to forget how sparkly and quirky those little uneven things are?

"Well howdy, pretty ladies," Jack says gregariously. "What brings you to the Blue Ridge Roast today?" I can tell by the cadence of his voice he's playing one of his little games.

"We heard there were the friendliest baristas in town here," I say with a toothy grin. Margot taps the counter with her fingers like she's already bored with our game.

"So, are you two sweethearts local or are you visiting Black Mountain?" Jack asks playfully.

"My cousin here is from Charlotte," I answer in an exaggerated Southern accent. "But I came all the way from Music City USA."

"Nashville, eh?" Jack has moved on to an old-time reporter voice. "You know, the love of my life was from Nashville. Maybe you know her."

"Okay, that's enough from you, Crawley." Margot crosses her arms.

"Always a pleasure to see you, Margot," Jack says as he leans over the counter and kisses her on the cheek. Then he pauses, leaning into me, and says, "And it's an extra pleasure to see you, Avery." He kisses my cheek too.

We order our coffee, and Jack promises he'll come sit with us when he gets a break. I head toward my favorite green velvet chair, and as I sit, Margot gives me an "I told you so" look.

"You better get that townie of yours under control," she says in a no-nonsense tone. I'm worried she might be right. Was he flirting or was he being Jack? Eventually, he takes a break and joins us as promised.

"So where's Andy?" Margot asks when Jack sits on the edge of my chair.

"He has class today," Jack answers. "But you can come by my house and see him anytime you want. He stays with us now."

"I'm so glad he was able to go back to art school," I say.

"Is he still with Spencer?" Margot asks.

"Don't think so. It flamed out when Spencer started college," Jack says. "I think that's pretty normal. When people go off to college, the relationship doesn't usually last, you know?"

This comment feels a little too on the nose to be unintentional. He must be on the same page as I am. We're back to being friends.

"Avery, can we talk outside for a minute?" he asks.

I avoid looking at Margot and follow him to the same bench where we broke up this summer. "What's up?"

"I'm playing a set Friday night at the Blue Ridge, and I really want you to come."

"Why did we need to come outside to talk about that?"

"Margot is shooting me dirty looks. I didn't really want her weighing in if you and I should hang out or whatever," he says while running his fingers through his hair.

"Fair enough." I nod.

A bell chime goes off, and Jack pulls his phone out of his black apron. "That's the alarm for my break," he says. "I've got to get back to work."

"What am I looking at there, Crawley?" I point at the phone in his hands. "Where is your trusty old flip phone?"

"Playing sets and getting tips has its perks," he answers as he tucks the new iPhone in his apron. He takes a small step closer to me. "Please say you'll come Friday. It would mean so much to me for you to see what a good gig I have going here."

I give him a half-smile. "I'll be there."

"God, it's good to see you," he says and takes one more step, inching even closer. Then he puts his arms around me and hugs me tight.

As he hugs me, I realize how much my body missed his body. I missed those strong arms and his chest, which feels so solid when I rest my head in its grooves.

I miss how when we hug we fit together like the last two puzzle pieces.

He finally lets go, and then swallows hard, like he wants to say something. But he doesn't. He heads back to work his shift, and Margot and I finish our drinks then walk home.

On the way, I'm quiet, while Margot fills the air with some story about the best bar in Coconut Grove. I'm only half listening.

I can't stop thinking that not only don't I not know where Jack's head is at when it comes to him and me, I'm not really sure where my head is at either.

CHAPTER THIRTY-EIGHT

Friday, October 21ˢᵗ

It's a chilly October night, so Margot and I borrow the Yukon to drive to the Blue Ridge Roast. I'm not sure what to expect, so I keep it simple with dark skinny jeans, a white sweater, and a tan motto jacket. When Margot and I walk in, we look at each other. We're shocked by the vibe. The lights are dimmed, and the coffeehouse has a completely different atmosphere than it does during the day. Our favorite chairs are taken, so we pick a little table near the small stage. Daisy, a Blue Ridge waitress, brings us a beer list. I recognize her from the summer. She was in the café the day I met Andy, but then was on vacation the rest of the time I was in Black Mountain.

"Blue Ridge serves booze now?" Margot asks excitedly as she looks over the menu.

Daisy laughs and says, "Try something from Highland Brewing Company."

Margot tells her, "Surprise me."

I order a Diet Coke.

"Y'all ever heard Jack Crawley play before?" Daisy asks us. "You're in for a real treat, you know."

"He's a friend actually," I say, and I can't help but beam with a little pride.

Jack emerges from the kitchen, wearing a black muscle tank top and his standard ripped jeans.

When Daisy brings us our drinks, I take her in from head to toe. Her hair is the perfect shade of light red, straight and shiny. She has green eyes, impossibly white teeth, and moves through the café with an effortless belonging.

When Jack said he and I were too different to ever work out, is this who he had in mind? Her aura sparkles with feathery happiness, and right now my own aura can best be described as a thud of heavy grief.

When Jack starts to play though, I forget about Daisy and my grief. I can't take my eyes off the little stage. Jack is perched so naturally on his stool. I've never seen him more in his element. The whole crowd is putty in his hands as he strums out melodies and croons. Della must be so proud. I don't think I could be any happier watching him shine like this, but then he takes it up a notch.

"I hope y'all don't mind if I take off the guitar for a minute," he says into the microphone. He gets off his stool and pulls the strap over his shoulder, then bends down to grab his violin out of its case. He points his bow right at me, then strings out a few notes of the *Doctor Who* theme song, before transitioning into "Kashmir" by Led Zeppelin.

Margot whistles through her fingers and I clasp my hands to my chest in pure delight. When he finishes the song, he pauses to put down his violin, and he picks up his guitar. While the music is stopped, I look around the café at how much fun his audience is having. It's then I spot it, and my happy glow drops.

From across the restaurant, Daisy blows Jack an undeniably seductive kiss. I see it. Margot sees it. Jack sees it, and flashes Daisy the same two-dimple smile he used to give me.

Without hesitation, Margot flags Daisy over to our table.

"Can we get the check?" Margot asks. "And can you please give Jack our apologies. We need to leave."

"Is everything okay?" Daisy asks, all kind and concerned.

"Our Gran took a bad fall," Margot says dramatically. "We have to get home right away." She lays some cash on the table, grabs my arm, and pulls me out of the café.

"You're welcome," Margot says as soon as we are on the other side of the door.

"You didn't have to do that."

"Of course I did. That was pure torture. Are you all right?"

"Why wouldn't I be?" I'm nearly screaming. "Jack clearly has a thing going on with Daisy. I have Henry. What's not to be happy about?"

"You don't have to be fake with me." Margot puts her arm around my shoulder, and my body finally feels like it has permission to let go of all of it.

I cry hard.

I cry for me.

I cry for Whit.

I cry for OCMC.

And I cry for Jack.

CHAPTER THIRTY-NINE

Saturday, October 22nd

Della finds out we're in town and invites Margot and me to dinner. Mom and Dad encourage us to go and promise they'll be okay without me for one meal.

The whole dinner gives me major *déjà vu* from last summer. The food is the same, Della's lively stories are the same, only the seating arrangement is different. I sit next to Andy, where Spencer used to sit, and Daisy, who's also been invited, sits next to Jack, where I used to sit.

Della serves my favorite banana pudding, and Jack plays karaoke violin for us. I spend most of the evening catching up with Andy about art school, and what it's like to live in an Elvis shrine. We are deep in conversation about life, and Andy is sharing big brotherly advice about college classes, when Jack interrupts.

"Can I borrow Avery for a second?" he asks then nods toward his bedroom. I feel a pit in my stomach thinking about the last time I was in there, but I follow him anyway. He shuts the door and gets a giddy look on his face. "I need to tell you something, but Della can't know."

"What?" It's unlike Jack to keep secrets from Della.

"My mom is driving through town tomorrow." He looks like a little boy on Christmas morning. "I'm going to go meet her at a diner off Route Forty at dinner time tomorrow night."

"Wow, that's big." I know he hasn't seen his mom since he was twelve. "How are you feeling?"

"Honestly, I'm really excited," he says. "She finished a really good rehab, and we've been texting some, and she seems really healthy. We're on fall break next week, so who knows? If dinner goes well, maybe she can spend some time here. Maybe you can even meet her."

"So why is something like that a secret from Della?"

He seems defensive when he says, "Della's always worried about me getting hurt. She doesn't trust my mom, so she'd think it's a bad idea. But I'm eighteen, it's not really up to Della."

I nod, even though I don't totally agree with that logic. "Promise to tell me all about it."

"Of course," he says then puts his hand on my shoulder. "I'm glad you're here and we're cool. I'm sorry that I kinda sprung Daisy on you. It's not serious or anything. We're like hanging out and stuff. I didn't know how to put that in an email, and then you sat at her table last night, and I never had a chance to explain."

"It's okay." I know now would be an ideal time to tell him about Henry, but things between Jack and me feel good, and I'm too afraid to mess with that. "Daisy's great. I'm happy for you."

He pulls on one of my braids and opens the bedroom door. When we rejoin the group on the porch, I can't help but notice Daisy is completely unfazed by the guy she's "hanging out with" whisking another girl away to his bedroom. She holds her head high with a type of confidence I could only ever dream of having.

When the night wraps up, and Jack hugs me tight to say good-bye, she doesn't even flinch. Daisy stays cool and confident.

Jack Crawley has found his match.

***

The next night, I'm already in bed and watching a movie on my phone when "Violin-Jack" lights up my screen. I don't even let it ring for a second. I can't wait to hear how the dinner with his mom went.

"Hello," I answer.

"Averrrry, my bee-you-teef-ful, sweet Averrry." He's sloshing and slurring on the other end.

"Jack, are you okay?" I sit up straight in the bed. Margot has headphones on and doesn't seem to notice me.

"I'm better than okay, Averrry. I'm perfect. Absa-fucking-lutely perfect," he stammers.

"Are you drunk?"

"I don't drink, Averrry. You know that. You know me better than fucking anybody." I make a mental note that Jack likes the F word when he's drunk.

"Where are you?" I'm in my pajamas. A pair of purple plaid flannel pants, and an old Warner Prep t-shirt, but I don't bother to change. I put on my sneakers, grab a hoodie, and wait for his answer.

"Under the Elvis wind chime, Averrry..." he slurs. "Elvis was an addict, you know. Probably stood up his kid all the time." I get it now. His mom didn't show for their dinner date.

I head out the sliding glass door and keep Jack on the phone while I walk to his house. While I walk, he tells me the whole sad story of waiting in a booth for three hours before finally accepting his mom wasn't going to show.

"I'm sure there's a good reason," I say. "Did you try to call her?"

"Phone goes straight to fuckin' voice mail."

When I reach the stone steps, I hang up. Jack is lying on the porch swing under the Elvis wind chime and a dozen beer bottles are beneath him. He sits up so I can join him on the swing, and then puts his head down in my lap.

"I'm so sorry," I say as I run my fingers through his hair out of habit. "I know how excited you were to see her."

"She's a good person, you know," Jack slurs.

"I know." I keep stroking his gorgeous, thick black hair to soothe him. My heart breaks seeing him so dejected. "Tell me something good about her."

"She likes names." He opens his eyes and looks up at mine. "If she was here, she could probably tell you the exact meaning and origin of Avery. And Jane. And Walker."

"I like that," I say. "So, what made her choose Jack for you?"

"My dad chose Jack. That was Della's brother's name. Mom chose my middle name. Campbell. It means crooked mouth." His eyes are closed again. "My dad had a super crooked smile, and my mom says that's why she fell for him. She hoped I would have one too, so she named me Jack Campbell."

I untwine my hands from his hair and put a finger in one of his crooked little dimples. "It worked."

We're quiet for a moment before he says, "I should've followed you when you walked away from the café after our fight. It's all I can think about sometimes. I regret it every day."

"You're drunk," I say, but my heart is warm. It feels good to hear those words, even if they're too late. "You don't mean that. You know, you probably should've called Daisy instead of me."

"I called you instead of Daisy for a reason. You're the best person I've ever known. I knew you'd get it. You've been through shit, you know?"

I nod and he keeps talking. "It's easy for Daisy to be fun and light because she hasn't been through the fucking shit people like you and me have been through. Plus, your hair smells like the beach, and I needed the beach tonight."

Jack starts tracing a line between three freckles on my thigh like he's connecting stars of a constellation. I try to imagine Henry doing the same thing. It would feel so out of place and awkward if Henry did it. But with Jack, it feels comfortable. "I was lost those few weeks we didn't talk."

I don't say anything. I let drunk Jack emote. Eventually, he's quiet, and we swing, me twirling his hair around my fingers, him drawing constellations with my freckles. He breaks the silence. "So what were you doing when I called?" His voice is a little less sloshy.

"I was already in bed," I say and gesture to my pajamas. "I was watching *Dead Poets Society*."

"That's so random, Walker," he says. "Even for you."

"Not really. It was Whit's favorite movie. I've been re-watching it more and more lately. I actually think it might be my Elvis. I watch it when I miss him."

"This whole year, you never told me that little fact about Whit," Jack says. "I've never heard of that movie though, what's it about?"

"You never had to watch it in English class?" I ask. "It's famous for all the kids standing on their desks and reciting a poem called 'O Captain! My Captain!' to Robin Williams. It's pretty cheesy. You'd probably hate it."

Jack looks like he is deep in thought trying to reimagine who Whit was. "You have such little faith in me. Believe it or not, I know that poem. It's the one secretly about Ol' Honest Abe keeling over, right?"

"That's the one."

Jack starts mumbling, "O Captain! My Captain!" out loud. He doesn't seem to know any other words, so he repeats these four over and over. He lifts his head out of my lap and sits up straight. Then he says the phrase again louder, right at me. "O Captain! My Captain!"

"You say it now, Avery," he directs me. I can't tell if he's drunk, or playing some game with me. Or maybe both. He's had a rough night, so I indulge him and say, "O Captain! My Captain!"

He repeats it one more time, but this time as he says the "O" he draws an "O" in the air with his finger. As he says "Captain" he draws a "C" in the air, an "M," and one more "C."

Holy crap. I get it now. OCMC was never anybody's initials. It's a reference to the Walt Whitman poem, or maybe *Dead Poets Society*. "This is huge," I shout, practically knocking him off the swing.

"We have to reopen the investigation, Detective Walker," he shouts back at me.

"We need to look for somebody who might have reminded Whit of the poem, or the movie," I say, my words barely able to catch up to my spinning thoughts. "Could be somebody who loved poetry, or maybe a girl named Chris, or Noel, or even Robin?" I start listing as many *Dead Poets Society* character names as I can remember.

"Does this mean you want to break into Black Mountain High School again and look through yearbooks?" Jack asks eagerly.

"Heck no. We're both eighteen. We can't risk that. There has to be another way to get our hands on some yearbooks."

"Of course." He reaches across the porch for his phone. "Daisy went to Black Mountain High, and so did her big sister, and her little sister. Between the three of them, they have to have a ton of yearbooks." He starts tapping away furiously on his phone, instructing Daisy to bring over all the yearbooks she can find in her house. When he's done typing, he holds my face in his hands and whispers, "We're going to find her, Avery."

When Daisy arrives, Jack is back to lying in my lap, and of course, Daisy doesn't bat an eye at this in the slightest. She hugs us both and tells us how excited she is we might find who we've been looking for. I hop up from the swing and move to a chair so Daisy can sit by her boyfriend. She's brought a big tote bag with six different years of Black Mountain High yearbooks.

"I think we should start by looking for poetry clubs," Jack says.

"You're brilliant," Daisy says and kisses him on the lips. I suddenly feel very out of place.

"I really need to get back to my gran's," I say. "My parents will notice if I'm missing for too long. Bring the yearbooks to Blue Ridge tomorrow, okay?" I stand and start to head to the steps.

"I'm going to walk Avery out," Jack says to Daisy, then follows me. When we reach the bottom of the stone stairs he says, "Hey. I know you think I'm drunk, but I meant every single word I said to you tonight." He doesn't give me a chance to respond before he heads up to the porch. To his girlfriend.

CHAPTER FORTY

Monday, October 24ᵗʰ

It's officially the first anniversary of Whit's death. I'm sure the grief books say I'm supposed to feel a certain way. Sad. Reverent. But the truth is I'm tired. Tired from grieving for 365 days. Tired from being up way too late for a quantum confusing night with Jack. I skip my morning run and wrap up in a warm blanket on the porch glider, sipping coffee. Today's also officially the first day of Warner Prep's fall break. I'm no longer missing any classes, and I let myself relax a little with a copy of *The Brain's Way of Healing*. Seems like an appropriate read given today's date. Mostly though, I'm trying not to think about last night.

I'm not on the porch for long when I hear footsteps coming down the gravel drive. My parents are on a hike, and Margot is still asleep.

I get off the glider and crane my neck to see whose feet are crunching the gravel.

So much for not thinking about last night.

There's Jack with his guitar slung over his shoulder, just like the night I re-met him at the bonfire, his heavy work boots churning the gravel beneath them. I walk down the steps and meet him halfway in the driveway.

"I thought the plan was for me to come to the Blue Ridge today during your shift and look at yearbooks later this afternoon." I'm still wearing my purple pajamas from last night, but with a yoga wrap. I pull it tight around my body, suddenly embarrassed about the lack of clothes.

"Good morning to you too, sunshine," he says. "Sorry for deviating from the plan."

"What's up?"

"I really wanted to thank you in person for coming over last night. I was really, really sad, and you made me feel better. So thanks."

"You're welcome. Sorry I was short with you right now. I'm surprised to see you here, I guess. Did you have a nice evening with Daisy?"

"No, not really." He looks up at the sky. "Actually, I broke up with Daisy last night."

"What? Really?" I'm completely surprised. "But she's great. Why would you break up with her?"

"I liked her a lot, and we had fun together, but it wasn't that serious," he says.

"But isn't that exactly what you want? Why did you break up with her, Jack?"

"Daisy *is* great. She's just not…she's not…" Jack looks up to the sky again, like he might find the answer in the clouds. Before he can say anything, car tires crunching up the gravel drive interrupt our conversation. We both look up, and there right in front of us is Henry's Prius, sneaking up on us in the way only a Prius can.

Henry. My boyfriend. Shit. I say nothing to Jack and rush to the door of the Prius. *You're the happy, albeit surprised girlfriend, doing nothing wrong,* I repeat in my head as Henry opens the door.

"Henry," I shout with a little bit too much enthusiasm. "What are you doing here?"

"Your gran invited me for fall break. I know it's going to be a hard day for your family. I wanted to surprise you, and maybe cheer you up," he says and pulls a bouquet of sunflowers out of the passenger seat. He puts his hand around my waist and pulls me in for a delicate kiss. Then, he looks to Jack, who's standing in the middle of the driveway with a bewildered look on his face. It's the first time since we were preteens I've seen Jack Crawley look awkward.

"Did I interrupt something?" Henry asks, looking back at Jack.

"No, no. Of course not." I don't even feel like I'm lying because I have no idea what was going on between me and Jack before Henry arrived.

"We got some new information for our investigation into who OCMC might be," I say, spitting the words out unnaturally fast.

"Oh," Henry says. "Then you must be the famous Jack. I've heard so much about you."

A switch flips on Jack's face. The bewilderment is replaced by the world's fakest smile. "And you must be the famous Henry," he says. "I've heard so much about you too." This is a lie. Jack has heard nothing about Henry.

"Well, nice to meet you," Henry says.

"Likewise," Jack returns.

I stand on my tiptoes and awkwardly swing my arms, unsure of what to say.

"I need to get to work, but I'll bring the yearbooks to the café with me," Jack says. "You should join us there to look through them, Henry."

"We'll be there," Henry says, wrapping his arms around me. Is he being territorial? Does he suspect something, or am I being paranoid? I can't quite tell.

Jack adjusts his guitar over his shoulder and walks down the driveway without looking back.

CHAPTER FORTY-ONE

Henry brings his suitcase into the cottage, and Gran directs him to stay in Whit's old converted porch bedroom. We spend some time sitting around the table watching Gran fawn over the word "Harvard" a few dozen times before heading to Blue Ridge Roast. Margot joins us. She says she'll be an extra set of eyes to sift through yearbooks, but I think she's hoping to see some drama unfold.

When we arrive, I go to the counter and Jack hands me the tote bag full of yearbooks. Andy spots us and comes over to meet Henry, and gives me a kiss on the cheek.

"No worries, Henry my man, Andy won't steal your girl," Jack says, putting his hands on Henry's shoulders as if to be sure the whole café knows Jack stands a good foot taller than Henry, who looks confused by the whole scene.

"Andy's gay," I whisper, so Henry can catch up.

I sit in my favorite green velvet chair and spread out the yearbooks on the coffee table. There are six from Black Mountain High School, and one from Asheville Arts Academy. I hold it up.

"That's Andy's," Jack says. "I grabbed it out of his room this morning. I figured it couldn't hurt."

"Oh. Fun," I say. "I think I'll start here."

Andy walks over quickly when he sees me holding it up. "Please don't, Aves. I'll die of embarrassment. I wasn't as cool as you kids when I was in high school."

"Oh come on, look at me," I say. "You have nothing to be embarrassed about." I start flipping to find the "L" section, to find Andy.

"No really. Don't," Andy says insistently. He's looking at the book like he might snatch it out of my hands. But I'm already on his page, so of course, I'm going to look.

I use my finger to scan down to his picture. There is nothing particularly embarrassing about it. It looks like a generic senior tuxedo headshot. A younger version of Andy stares back at me from the page, then my eyes scan over to his name, which is written in yearbook style: Last Name, First Name. Lincoln, Anderson.

The word "Lincoln" pops off the page, each letter burning in my eyes. I can hear Jack's voice from last night in my head: "Isn't that the poem about Ol' Honest Abe?"

I always imagined solving the mystery of OCMC would be a slow process. If I ever tried to picture it in my head, I envisioned myself standing in front of a big wall with little clues pinned up, and strands of red yarn connecting the clues in a big messy web. I thought I would study the wall, and after hours and hours of looking at it, the answer would slowly, but steadily, come into focus.

But this is not at all what it's like.

It happens all at once, like a lightning bolt. There's no more wondering. No more deep thinking. The whole mystery makes perfect sense in a single flash.

Andy is staring at me, his pupils huge, and I notice his lips are quivering.

"Was my brother in love with you, Andy?" I ask angrily through gritted teeth.

Everybody else around the coffee table, who hasn't had the lightning bolt of understanding, looks shocked. Jack's jaw is hanging open, and Margot covers her face with her hands.

This isn't the type of drama she was hoping for.

Henry looks like he is trying to keep up.

Andy doesn't say anything, so I ask again. "Was my brother in love with you, Anderson Lincoln?"

He finally nods. It feels like the café is spinning around me.

I know I should be happy.

I've figured out a puzzle that's been haunting me for an entire year.

But instead of happiness, I feel betrayed.

I thought Andy was my friend. I thought he had my best interests at heart when he told me to stop searching last summer. My expression must show my disgust and hurt.

"I'm so sorry I didn't tell you," Andy says through tears.

Without thinking I stand, grab my bag, and stomp my way to the door. Out of the corner of my eye, I can see Henry and Andy are trying to follow me. But one by one Jack puts his hand on their shoulders, pulling them back to the coffee table.

"Let me take care of this," he says in a low growl.

Henry looks offended, but I don't care.

Jack reaches me as the door dings shut and pulls me into his big body and he doesn't say a word. I'm so thankful for him.

We say nothing. He takes my hand and leads me to the little alley where nobody can see us. He looks so sad too, and I remember Andy is his best friend. Jack's been as invested in solving this mystery as I was.

I can't think of anything to say, so I lean my head against his chest and listen to his heartbeat. I can tell he is processing because of the way he kind of swings back and forth on his heels.

After a few minutes, he puts his hand under my chin and tilts my head up so I'm looking at him. "Are you upset because OCMC is a guy?"

"Of course not," I answer quickly and firmly. "I'm upset because OCMC is my friend."

"Listen." He takes a deep breath and I can feel it in my own body: we're standing that close. "Andy is a good guy. You know that, right?" I nod. "I don't know why he didn't tell us. Jesus, I wish he had, but I am sure he had a reason, you know?"

I stay quiet.

"I think you should hear him out," Jack says. "You owe it to yourself to know the whole truth, and I trust Andy."

I sigh, and then say, "Okay, go get him."

I follow Jack out of the alley and watch as he opens the door and goes in to talk to Andy, who's apparently disappeared into the kitchen. While they're talking, Henry gets up and comes outside to find me. I assume he's going to take his turn to comfort me through my shocking news, but I'm wrong.

He comes outside, shaking his head, and his cheeks are unnaturally red. "Is something going on between you and Jack?" he asks in a whisper-shout.

"I don't know," I say honestly.

"Well, do you have feelings for him?"

All the patterns of my life shift through my brain.

My grandmother denying our family's tragedy. Everybody putting on a show. My brother hiding his true self. Hiding who he loved.

I can't do it.

I have to break the pattern.

I have to be honest.

Who the fuck cares if Henry is perfect on paper? It's not the truth. Jack uses the F word when he's drunk. I use it when I make honest breakthroughs.

"Yes," I answer quietly. "I'm pretty sure I do."

"I'm not interested in competing in some love triangle," Henry says. "Good luck, Avery." He doesn't wait for me to reply and heads toward his Prius, driving off as quietly as he arrived.

CHAPTER FORTY-TWO

Andy comes out of the Blue Ridge Roast by himself and finds me in the alley, leaning against the brick wall. "Where do you want me to start?" he asks.

I don't hesitate. "Start with what Whit was going to tell me that night."

"He was going to tell you he wasn't going to sign with a school. He wanted to go somewhere he could be himself, be with me, and study poetry."

"Wow." Even though I'd figured most of that out on some level, it's still surreal to hear it out loud.

"You know that green velvet chair you love?"

"Yeah."

"Well, your brother loved that chair too. That's where he was sitting when we met." He takes a deep breath and the story rolls out of him like it's been held captive in his mind for years, and is finally free.

"About two years before he died, Whit had finished his sophomore year, and I had graduated high school and gotten a job at Blue Ridge Roast. He used to sneak away every morning to get coffee and read his poetry books. Tennyson. Thoreau. Frost." The memory makes Andy smile. "He was such an enigma to me. This big, broad bro in football shirts reading poetry. I had to talk to him. Once I started talking to him, I couldn't stop. We clicked in the right ways. I know you know what that feels like."

Andy pauses, choosing his words carefully. "He was always," he holds his thumb and forefinger a half inch apart, "this close to telling you and your parents about me. He wanted more time to figure out how someone like me fit into his world. You know better than anybody what the pressure was like for him."

I nod. Boy do I know.

"Remember the time he went to a training camp in Atlanta over spring break his junior year?"

"I think so."

"There was no camp." Andy grins sheepishly. "We spent a whole week together where we could be a couple. It was the best week of my life. I really loved him so much, Aves. And he loved me too."

"I wish I would've known all this sooner. I wish you could've been there for his funeral and grieved with us." I shake my head. "You told Jack and me you bet OCMC Googled Whit and found his obituary. Was that true? Is that how you found out he died?"

"Yeah, it's true." Little tears roll down Andy's brown cheeks. "At first I thought he changed his mind. I never thought he stopped loving me, but I thought maybe your parents found out about me, or his coach found out about me, and maybe Whit had to play it cool for a while. Every once in a while, I'd text him to see if he was ready to talk again, and then one day you texted back."

"You blocked me, Andy," I say, remembering the moment.

"I had to, Aves," he says. "Whit was so insanely private about our relationship. I knew if you had his phone something must've gone wrong. That's when I Googled him. There were hundreds and hundreds of hits. So many tributes to this beloved high school football legend. It felt wrong to change the way people saw him. I couldn't out him when he wasn't there to have a say in it."

"That's why you didn't tell me." I recall the first day I walked into the café and met Andy, and the way he looked at me like he knew me. I always assume everything is about Jack. It wasn't about Jack at all. It was about Whit all along.

"Can you ever forgive me, Aves?"

"You always call me Aves instead of Avery," I say. "How did I never notice that?"

"Well, Whit used to talk about you a lot, and that's what he called you so that's how I think of you. As Aves."

Now, we're both crying.

I hug Andy hard. Finding Whit's mystery love did not go down at all like I expected, but when I hug Andy, solving the puzzle is everything I ever imagined it to be. I feel like I have a tiny piece of Whit in my arms. I might actually know Whit better in this moment than I ever did while he was on Earth.

"Whit would want us to be friends," I say. "Of course, I forgive you."

"Can I stop by your gran's house after my shift tonight?"

"Sure," I say.

"I have something I want to give you," he says. "It's something I've been holding on to for a long time, but I think it really should belong to you."

CHAPTER FORTY-THREE

Margot and I have to walk home. We rode into town with Henry, who is long gone by the time we get back.

"How are you feeling about all this?" she asks.

"I don't know. It's so much to take in. Whit and Andy. Did you have any idea?"

"No. That's not what I mean," she says. "Whit and Andy, woohoo, that's all fine and good. But I meant do you want to talk about how Jack is the one who followed you out of the store and held you while you cried? Henry drove off in his Prius with that stupid Harvard bumper sticker while Jack was there for you."

"I don't know what there is to say. Do I love Jack? Probably. But all the reasons he said we don't belong together are still true."

"I will never understand you two," she says.

***

After dinner, Andy stops by and I meet him at the end of the driveway on the brick culvers so we can talk privately. I don't know yet what I am going to do with this information about Whit. But I do know for sure I'm not quite ready to share the news with the whole family. Andy pulls a black Moleskine journal out of his messenger bag and hands it to me. I open it and feel a rush of warmth come over me as I see Whit's handwriting. His jagged, jock-like letters fill the lined pages of the little journal, and I feel like I'm looking at an old friend.

"So. Whit didn't just read poetry," Andy explains. "He wrote it too." I flip through the journal and see page after page of love poems written from Whit to Andy. After each poem, there is a delicate drawing in Andy's artistic style.

"He'd write the poems and I'd illustrate them."

"I can't possibly keep this, Andy." I continue flipping through, each page more beautiful than the last. There are sketches of two boys holding hands, one in a number eight jersey and one in a barista apron. There's a drawing of the view from Graybeard's Point. There are more abstract drawings like one with tree roots wrapped around each other and growing together.

At the end of the journal, there's an angel sitting on a cloud looking over Black Mountain.

"I need you to keep it, Aves," he says. "I will always love Whit, but it's time for me to start to heal and move on. Now that the truth is finally out in the universe, I feel like I can finally do it. I need you to keep the journal."

I hold the book tight to my chest. "I will treasure this forever."

"You know how you said Whit would want us to be friends?"

"Yes," I answer and wipe a tear from my cheek.

"I think he'd also like it if I offered you some big brother advice." I know exactly where Andy is going. "Aves, I loved Whit so much, and then I woke up one day and he was gone. Every single day I wonder if I should have pushed him to be public about our relationship. I hate I never got to show the world how much I loved him, and then it was too late."

I kick my feet on the culver, thinking about what Andy is saying.

"It's not too late for you," he says. "I know it's cheesy, but guess what? Your brother had a really cheesy side to him. For Christ's sake, his favorite movie was *Dead Poets Society*. I think at first he only liked me because he couldn't believe my name was actually Anderson Lincoln."

I laugh remembering the cheesy side of Whit.

"If Whit were here, I really think his big brother's advice to you would be *carpe diem*, Aves."

I stand up on the stone culver as though I'm the fictional Todd Anderson standing on his desk. "Okay," I say. "Let's do it."

"Wait. What?" Andy asks. "Are you serious? Did that speech really work?"

"You're not too shabby at the whole big brother thing. Whit would be quite impressed," I tell him. "Now, walk with me to eighty-eight Oakley Road."

CHAPTER FORTY-FOUR

"You're on your own now, Aves," Andy says when we reach the bottom of the stone steps.

"One more thing," I say then I pull Whit's phone out of my hoodie pocket. "I'll keep your poetry book if you keep this. I need to heal and start my next chapter too."

"Are you sure?" Andy asks.

"The last text Whit ever sent was to you. He was thinking about you the last time he held this. It belongs with you, Andy." I hand him the phone, and he clutches it tight, holding back tears. I start to walk away, but he reaches for my arm and pulls me back to him. He wraps his arms around me and kisses my forehead. I give him a nervous nod, and then turn back to the stone stair steps that lead the way to Jack's house.

I climb them slowly, one by one, practicing my big "seize the day" speech in my head. When I reach the porch, I can hear an Elvis record playing loudly on the old record player inside.

Della must be in the living room and I don't really want to make small talk with her. Now that I know what I want to say to Jack, I want to say it right now.

I glance down the porch at Jack's bedroom window, and it is cracked open. I remember all the nights I spent climbing through it, and suddenly it seems like a good romantic gesture to climb through it once more.

It's cracked open about the width of two cups of coffee. I try to open it more, but it doesn't budge. In my memory, it was easier to jiggle open. I eye the opening again and decide I can probably manage to get through if I bend the right way.

You can do this, Avery. Remember you are a certified badass. I fold in half in a way that would make my yogi mother proud, and get about halfway through the opening before I hear laughter coming from behind me.

"What in god's name are you doing, Walker?" Jack asks between belly laughs, dimples popping. He pulls on my hips and helps me un-shimmy my way out of the window and back onto the porch.

"I heard Elvis," I say. "I thought Della was here, so was sneaking in. It was stupid, I know."

"Della's not here," Jack says. My hair is messy and wild from my window shimmying, so Jack pushes the strands out of my face, and pushes them behind my ears. "And please don't call yourself stupid again."

"So you're listening to Elvis alone then, Crawley?" I ask teasingly.

"He's an icon for a reason." Jack grins. Then I grin. Our gazes lock, and I know he knows why I'm here.

"Listen, Jack," I try to start my speech, but he takes a finger and puts it to my lips.

"Shhh," he says. "Dance with me, Walker."

"I need you to hear this," I protest. "I'm sorry I cared more about what my parents would think of you than what I felt for you. I wish Whit wouldn't've worried about what people would think, and would've followed his heart. I don't want to make the same mistake he did."

"That was a pretty good speech, darlin'," he says. "Can you dance with me now?" He puts one hand on my hip and holds my hand in the other. Then he spins me gracefully around the porch as Elvis's voice fills the air all around us.

"I'm not done," I say, but keep swaying with him, dancing slowly to the song. "I love you, Jack. I'm in love with you."

"I know that," he says with a smug grin, framed by his ridiculously crooked dimples.

"Can you not be so cocky for like one minute?" I know he is playing with me. We've grown up, but he's still Jack.

He brushes my hair away from my face again, so he can put his lips right to my ear. "Avery, I've loved you every day since I was thirteen years old. I was in love with you then, and I'm even more in love with you now."

He keeps spinning me slowly around the porch, and as we dance, I can feel the timid tween versions of Avery and Jack twirling right alongside us. I might not remember all the details of each little moment that got me from that shy girl to this version of myself, but I know Jack was with me.

He sings along to the lyrics of the song, whispering them in my ear. "Take my hand. Take my whole life too, for I can't help falling in love with the reminiscence bump."

I pull back and look at him. "That's not the lyric."

"I know," he says. "I meant I think this will be one. This song will give me the reminiscence bump someday."

I put my head against his chest, and he keeps talking. "You know what I mean, the reminiscence bump. It's the term neurologists use when a song changes your brain and imprints a moment in time. Some science nerd taught me about it."

"The reminiscence bump," I say back.

Then he leans down and kisses me long and deep, and full of love.

ABOUT THE AUTHOR

Elise lives in Nashville with her husband and three small children. She studied journalism at the University of Miami, and earned her Masters of Education from Harvard University. When she isn't writing, or wrangling children, she's planning adventures to National Parks.

Connect with Elise:

website: elisefender.com

twitter: @EliseWritesYA

FB: /EliseFenderAuthor

IG: @authorEliseFender

www.BOROUGHSPUBLISHINGGROUP.com

If you enjoyed this book, please write a review. Our authors appreciate the feedback, and it helps future readers find books they love. We welcome your comments and invite you to send them to info@boroughspublishinggroup.com.

Follow us on TikTok, Twitter, and IG. And be sure to sign up for our newsletter for surprises and new releases from your favorite authors.

Are you an aspiring writer? Check out www.boroughspublishinggroup.com/submit and see if we can help you make your dreams come true.

Love podcasts? Enjoy ours at www.boroughspublishinggroup.com/podcast.

Made in the USA
Coppell, TX
23 January 2022

72219769R00132